I, JACK

INTERPRETER'S NOTE

Speaking as Jack's real Pack Lady and interpreter, I would like to make certain things clear.

Firstly, although most of the animals are real, ALL OF THE PEOPLE ARE INVENTED AND SO IS THE STORY ITSELF.

There is no such place as South Cornwall, nobody is trying to build a motorway through it and there are no such people as the Stopes family – although there may be accidental resemblances to some of Jack's Packmembers. I'm afraid the Pack Lady in the story is a lot smaller, slimmer and more patient than me.

Jack is a Real Dog and has certainly helped me with this book, by lying on my feet until all circulation is cut off and helpfully bringing me one-legged Spiderman toys and dreadful socks.

The Cats are real and just as superior: their full names are Remillard (Remy), Amazon (Maisie) and Musketeer (Muskie).

Petra is real, but she belongs to a lovely family and I'm sorry to say Jack has never been given the chance to become her Packleader, although he would definitely like to.

It would be churlish and dishonest if I failed to acknowledge my immense debt to other writers about animals – particularly Rudyard Kipling whose very odd book *Thy Servant, A Dog* was the inspiration I needed to find Jack's own voice. Thanks also to Hazel Orme, the copy-editor on another book of mine, who first suggested it. Bruce Fogle's books about dog psychology have helped me to ground Jack's character in real dog-behaviour – which makes much better sense once you realize they're just domesticated wolves.

Finally, I would like to thank my daughter Alex and her class at Devoran Primary School in Cornwall who long ago helped me to think out the plot.

Patricia Finney

I, Jack

by Jack Perry

as told to Patricia Finney

illustrated by Peter Bailey

CORGI YEARLING BOOKS

to my Supper Dish ♥ ♥ ♥

**Find out more about Jack
on www.gooddogjack.co.uk**

I, JACK
A CORGI YEARLING BOOK : 0 440 864402

First publication in Great Britain

PRINTING HISTORY
Corgi Yearling edition published 2000

3 5 7 9 10 8 6 4

Set in 12/16pt Palatino
by Phoenix Typesetting, Ilkley, West Yorkshire.

Corgi Yearling Books are published by Transworld Publishers,
61–63 Uxbridge Road, London W5 5SA,
a division of The Random House Group Ltd,
in Australia by Random House Australia (Pty) Ltd,
20 Alfred Street, Milsons Point, Sydney, NSW 2061, Australia,
in New Zealand by Random House New Zealand Ltd,
18 Poland Road, Glenfield, Auckland 10, New Zealand
and in South Africa by Random House (Pty) Ltd,
Endulini, 5a Jubilee Road, Parktown 2193, South Africa.

Made and printed in Great Britain by
Cox & Wyman, Reading, Berkshire

CONTENTS

MY PACK AND OUR DEN

Hi! HI THERE! Hello! HI, FRIEND!! I am Jack! Look at me! Here I am. I like you. Do you like me? I am JACK. BIG DOG JACK!! Hi! Can I smell your . . . ?

Oh. Sorry.

I am Jack, old-fashioned yellow Labrador. I am very Thick. I am very very Thick. It's good to be Thick. WAG TAIL. Pant. Get patted. Thick means Good.

I have a big Pack, very big Pack, all different kinds of dog.

One kind of dog – standing-up-on-back-legs-type

smell-of-ape dog with no fur, no tail. Some big, some little. Apedogs.

Other kind of dog – normal-walking-type dog with fur, hidden claws.

And me.

Here is my Pack.

Front paw. Biggest standing-up apedog is Master and Packleader. He is very very Big (bigger than you). He has a big deep bark. He has a big belly, lots of dark fur on face (not much on head). He makes things with his clever paws in his little wooden den: sometimes he makes lines on paper with burnt sticks, or he puts lots of different-smelling slime on bits of paper, or he makes huge things out of wet earth. I get much whacking when I eat paper-with-smears even though the smell is so interesting. But whatever he does is Good because he is my Packleader and also Tom Stopes, also Dad. He is the biggest apedog. I love him HUGE AMOUNTS. More than steak, even.

🐾: **Other front paw.** Next biggest apedog is Pack Lady of my Pack,   also Charlie-short-for-Charlotte,   also Mum, also Darling. She is not as big as the Packleader (in fact she is quite little) but she barks higher and even more. She has no fur on face, lots of dark fur on head. She is **SCARY FIERCE** sometimes if she finds you with head-in-dustbin. I love her BIG AMOUNTS. More than pork chops.

🐾: **Back paw.** Apedog puppy bitch. She is nearly big now. She is Teresa, or Terri. She has no fur on face, fur on head, cuddles me. She has a box with loud howling and banging inside. She sits next to it and howls. Why does she get mad when I help with howling? I do not understand. I love her A LOT. More than kidneys.

Other back paw. Immature male apedog puppy. Smaller than Terri. No fur on face, short fur on head, runs around barking lots. Sits on two-wheel-go-fast-thing WATCH OUT JACK — YOU STUPIDOG. He is good to cuddle. He helps me dig for bones. Often he gives me Sugar Puffs and bits of toast and peanut butter — funny, sticky – but nice taste. He is called Pete. I love him a HUGE LOT. More than cow-liver, even.

Tail. Other male apedog puppy. Small. Very small. Was smaller. First he was a roly-poly no-fur puppy, getting milk from Pack Lady — NO, NOT FOR YOU, JACK. Why not? Anyway, now he is standing-up-type apedog, but short. He is friendly. When I kiss him, he licks my face. He is called Mikey and also Baba. I love him LOTS. More than chicken.

There are also normal-walking-with-fur-and-tail but small and hidden-claws. YOWP! They don't like me smelling their tails. We have lots. Stripy one, Remy. Black-and-white one, Maisie. White-and-black one, Muskie. More paws than I've got. Too many paws. Too hard. I love them a bit. Funny-looking dogs.[1]

There are also lots of Small Furries outside. Also Slimys in pond JUMP JUMP YOWP! Also Flying Featheries that cats make into meat and leave on kitchen floor and Pack Lady stands on half of in the morning and runs around barking and howling LOTS and throwing cats through the back door. I do not understand why cats make Flying Feathery and Furry friends into meat, but they say they like it and I am too Thick to live and what do I think I eat anyway?

Yes. I am Thick. I am very Thick. I am the thickest Dog in the World.

I will tell you about my Pack's den. It is good but Pack Lady says it's too small. Great Packleader and Pack Lady share a room, nice nest, why can't I come in it?

---

[1]   Actually, We are Cats. Signed, *The Cats*.

11

Too SMALL, YOU GREAT NERK, says Pack Lady.

Now the FOOD ROOM where my FOOD DISH is. My Food Dish is very beautiful. It is shiny and smooth and smells of metal. It has food in it both front paws times each day, one after sleep, one before  sleep. I LOVE MY FOOD DISH VERY MUCH. I can hold it in my mouth and carry it. Sometimes I drop it on Packleader's foot when he might forget about FOOD FOR THE DOG. He barks lots. Sometimes I drop it on the Food Room floor, bang kerlang CRASH! Good noise. Sometimes I get mixed up and fetch my water dish . . . Doing! Splosh! . . . I wonder how all that puddle happened?

Oh, sorry.

There is also the Sitting Room with the talking Flicker Box and a little room with another talking Flicker Box and a big wood-and-metal pling-plong noise-thing in it. Cats walk on it sometimes, to make beautiful music (they say). Sitting Room is nice. The Cats have their god in there. It is yellow and red and hot and makes a burning hot smell. I like it. Cats like it more. Why do they scowl at me when I lie next to it? They could lie on top of me and we would all be

12

warm and comfy. Why should Cats lie near the God and not me? I do not understand.

There is also Outside and Outside Outside. Outside has lots of trees and flowers and green things. I can do my messages there. Outside Outside is for Walkies. I LOVE WALKIES. CAN WE GO NOW! NOW! PLEASE! WALKIES NOW PLEASE?

Oh. Sorry.

Pack Lady does not like the den. She barks: it is A Pit. I like it. It smells lovely. All the floor-furs smell especially lovely because of when I was a puppy and didn't understand about Doing Messages Outside. Also because of smallest boy puppy not understanding this. (Why do apedogs do Messages in a Big White Waterdish? It wastes the lovely smell and makes it hard to lick respectfully. I do not understand.) Also there are even more interesting smells in the floor-furs because of Cats making Small Furries into meat on it. Also because of food I can't lick up. Also because of Packleader's smeary things. They are beautiful floor-furs, so full of nice smells.

Anyway, that is our Pack's territory. The Cats say, *Floor-furs are carpets for Cats to sit On if We want. Also, it is actually Our territory, but we allow the apecats and the Big Stupid to live there if they are useful to Us.*

And now I will tell you about my new Packmember. She is my friend. She is very beautiful. I love her MASSIVE GREAT HUGE AMOUNTS.

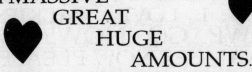

More than any Food at all, even birthday cake and gravy, even.

GIRL DOG!

Cats say, *The Big yellow Stupid doesn't know anything, we will help him tell this story.*[1]

Next to our den is another den. Sad den. No Pack there.

Then a Kennel That Moves[2] came – but it was HUGE. Like a Den That Moves. New apedogs came. Just a Pack Lady and her Packleader. No puppies yet. They did things, made it all new. Much funny-smelling smeary-stuff[3] on walls. Much wood smelling (mostly pine).

---

[1] Like this. Down here, dummies.
[2] Car, warm for sitting on. Eats hedgehogs. Big eyes at night.
[3] Called paint by the apecats, it is nasty, smelly and pointless and when it gets on Our fur it makes a horrible mess. We knock over pots of it whenever We can.

My Packleader barked over the fence to the new other NotMyPack apedog.

'Hi. How's it going?'

'Oh, you know how it is. Half of Letitia's Wedgwood collection got smashed. One of the tables was chipped. Nightmare, really.'

'I know.'

Other apedog made tooth-showing friendly-face.[1]

I said, *Hello, hi, how are you?* I stood up, paws on fence. Pant pant. Wag wag. Other apedog made friendly smell, friendly face. Ruffled my head, Oh Oh, stroked my ears I LIKE HIM, HE IS OK, HE LIKES ME. WAG TAIL LOTS.

---

[1] The Big Stupid means a smile, the apecats' (uncouth) equivalent of slowly-shutting-eyes.

'Hi there,' said other apedog. 'You're a handsome dog.'

'His name's Jack.'

'Well, hi there, Jack. Sorry, no biscuits.'

I know he's got no biscuits (sad sad why not?). But I can smell he has them in his removable fur sometimes. And . . . and . . .

OH WOW! I CAN SMELL ANOTHER DOG. A GIRL DOG. HE HAS A PRETTY FURRY GIRL DOG – quite young, very clean, neat delicate paws, very very pretty and clever, likes to eat choc drops and biscuits . . . OH WOW THIS IS GREAT!

'Hey, Jack, get down.'

'It's OK. He can probably smell my Samoyed bitch, Petra.'

Boy puppies Pete and Mikey came out, being NEEOOWW things, ran round the Outside NEEEEEOOOOOWWWW, fell into overgrown bushes FIGHT FIGHT. They barked and yip-yipped.

Other apedog was startled. 'Ah, you've got kids as well, then?' he said.

'You could put it that way.'

'Er . . . yes. Well, I'm John.'

'Hi, John. I'm Tom.'

They did touching-paws-friendly thing. Then the other apedog looked sadly at his paw. It was smeary.

Packleader coughed. 'Er . . . sorry. I've been painting all morning.' Packleader offered a lovely complex-smelly cloth from his leg-covering pocket. Ooh wow! A HALF-BISCUIT FELL OUT ON THE GROUND . . . SCRUNCH scrunch, yum yum. HAPPY DOG. But the other apedog did not like the lovely cloth. Tried to wipe his painty hand on leg-coverings, then stopped. Tried on leaves. Tried on fence. Sighed lots. His body said: *Yuk, horrid*. He was sad and went away.

Next thing was weird things Next Door. Apedog people everywhere, walking on the roof like cats stalking Feathery Friends.[1] Why?

WHEN WILL THE BEAUTIFUL GIRL DOG COME BACK? All the next-door apedog things smell of her. She is Nearly Ready. She is a little smaller than me and she likes liver and gravy

---

[1] Only not so beautiful, of course. Or graceful. Or like Us at all, in fact.

and Pedigree Chum and going for Walkies, but not puddles. She is very particular and likes to be clean. I think she has lots and lots of fur. Her paws make such delicate smell-prints. Oh oh. She is so lovely. WHERE IS SHE? WHEN WILL SHE COME BACK?

Then John Next Door did banging on long bits of wood. Then he did banging to hold wire on. Then his Pack Lady called Letitia went off in her car.

Vroom. Here is next-door Pack Lady's car again. Beautiful wonderful SMELL.

SHE'S HERE, ARROOF ARROOF, BEAUTIFUL GIRL DOG IS HERE! Snfff. She had Butchers' Dog Tripe and Liver for supper last night and Tesco mixer. She is younger than me. She is a little plump from not enough Walkies. She has been in a sad place, Oh OH, sad hard place with other dogs, and wire walls, and horrid clean smell every morning to hide nice Messages. I don't like that sad hard place.

But now she is HAPPY DOG. She is leaping in the back of the car. She is jumping up and down. She says, *Hi, hi, I'm Petra, hi. Oh hi there, you smell nice, what a Big Dog you are, respect respect, you live here, right? Can I come in? I like you.*

I said lots. I danced for joy, all over the Outside. Letitia opened the car, put Petra's lead on. She

bounced. She is white. Very long fur. Pretty curved-over tail. Pretty eyes and ears and whiskers. So pretty.

My Packleader is here. He says, 'Hey, that's one beautiful dog. Isn't she gorgeous?'

OH YES, she is *GORGEOUS*, can I be her friend, can I can I?

Petra says, *Hi, I like you too, we can be friends!*

My Packleader barks more. He says friendly things to Petra. He has *I-like-you* sound in his bark. She hears, she wants to smell us, she pulls Letitia Next Door over the boring hard road, through the hedge, over the flowerbed. Letitia next door is yelping, 'No, no, no!' but Petra doesn't hear.

I smell her. She smells me. WAG TAIL WAG WAG WAG. She does a Wet Message, special for me, right there on the grass, only a bit on Letitia's paw-covering,[1] saying all about herself and how old she is and when she will be Ready and everything. I do one too, right on top. Packleader is trying not to laugh again and digging in his pocket. Letitia is mad at Petra. Why? Anyway, my Wet Message says

---

[1] Dogs are disgusting.

about how Big I am and how I'm a Dog and I love Petra and everything. It is a very splendid Message. Petra likes it. I am a Happy Dog. I lick her face. She licks me. I hold her nose in my mouth, show who is bigger. She wags tail, says, *I like you, can we play? Shall we chase?*

She goes yip, yip, slips out of her lead. I pull hard, Packleader lets go of collar. We run. We play.

We run again. Chase tails. OH OH WOW! Happy Dog. HAPPY DOG. Petra is My Friend. HAPPY HAPPY HAPPY!

'I think they like each other,' says Packleader.

'Mm,' says Letitia Next Door, still wiping Wet Message off her new paw-covering. 'I don't think it's very suitable. Petra has a pedigree, you know.'

'So does Jack. Jack's descended from four champions.'

'Yes,' said Letitia Next Door with not-true smile and body saying: *You are dirty and inferior, yuk yuk.* 'But Jack is just a Labrador and Petra is a Samoyed, after all.'

Packleader barks a big booming laugh which makes Letitia wince. 'Better tell 'em quick.'

Letitia's body says: *Run away, run away.* She grabs Petra's scruff as we run past, drags her round and through next-door new-gate and in next-door front door.

YIP YIP! says Petra. *That was fun.*

AROOF AROOF, YES YES!

I am a VERY HAPPY DOG.

WAG TAIL. PANT.

Happy sigh.

SAD DOG

Now Sad Dog. Petra and me are friends. I love her more than FOOD. I would give her all my Food and my bed and my mouth-happy squeaky thing. She is the most beautiful girl dog I have ever seen. But her Pack Lady doesn't like me. There is a big fence now, very strong. Petra's Pack Lady does not-true smiles to me while her body says: *Yuk* and also *Scared.* 'Good doggy,' she says in ape-barking, which is nice, but her body says: *Go away, dirty, yuk, horrid.*

I am very sad. Why does Petra's Letitia not like me? I am not dirty. I am quite clean. I have a bath some-

times. I like baths. I lick my paws and
tummy to make sure they are clean.
I go water-running in the Very
Big Funny Tasting Wet
That Goes Woosh
Woosh.[1] Letitia is too
clean and bony. When
does she eat? She should
eat more, maybe then she
would be happy. I am HAPPY DOG when
I eat.

I smell Petra through the fence. I smell Petra in the
back Outside. I smell Petra's Wet Messages when
we go for Walkies and once I found her Hard
Message hidden in a leafy bit. OH, I AM A
HAPPY DOG. Petra left me a present. Wag.
Sniff. Sniff. Wag. She ate Pedigree Chum and mixer
and choc drops and a biscuit. She is a beautiful girl
dog and I love her sooo much. Everywhere smells
of Petra.

I wish Packleader would not spoil my Hard
Messages by picking them up in crinkly plastic and
putting them in the dustbin. It is sad. That was a
present for Petra, not for Packleader. Oh well. Hard
Messages are very interesting for smelling: I understand why Packleader wants it.

---

[1] We think he means swimming in a very horrible nasty thing
called the Sea.

When I go to sleep in the dark time, I sniff hard at the Cats' little door,[1] get my nose all full of beautiful Petra girl-dog smells. Ahhhh.

BREAKFAST TIME!

Morning is Happy Time. Light comes back.

Trouble is, my tummy is E M P T Y. It goes gug gug gug. I am Terribly HUNGRY. Oh oh. Too too hungry.

But I mustn't howl. Never never howl. And I mustn't bark. No matter how terribly empty starving H U N G R Y. No matter how l o o o ng since supper . . .

SOOOO LOOOONG . . .

Never howl or bark or bad bad bad. 'Do you know what time it is? It's ruddy-well five in the morning! Bad dog, go to bed, bad bad bad!'

Then I am a Sad Dog.

It is soothing to chew things. Oh good, here is Pete's paw-covering, nice comfy smell of Pete and mud.

Strange round tick-tick thing upstairs goes 'Beep beep beep . . . click!'[1]

Creak upstairs. Thud thud. Creak creak creak, click, squerk. 'Uhhh.' I stand up. Oh so excited! Creak, Slither, rustle, rustle, creak. Thud thud thud . . .

HERE SHE IS! Here is Pack Lady! Yip yip yippee! Puppy bouncing. Happy puppy. Puppy dance. HAPPY DOG. *GOOD MORNING PACK LADY, RESPECT RESPECT.*

I am very Clever as well as Thick. I can talk ape-barking. Every morning when Pack Lady comes down the stairs she says, 'Oh, hello, Jack.'

And I say, in ape-barking: 'ERRO! ERRO! ERRO!' This is ape happy-morning bark. I can do it too.[2]

Then I say, *Hi, how are you, how lovely you smell, you are beautiful, where is my* FOOD, *let me smell your . . .*

---

[1] Fun to play with, though easy to kill. Not edible.
[2] We are afraid this is true. He sounds terrible.

And Pack Lady makes her happy-morning-bark which goes 'Geroff you stupidog,' and she gives me a lovely friendly push in my side.

I do much bouncy. I am

Happy

Happy Happy.

Soon Food.

Pack Lady staggers into the Food room. I dance round her, careful not to trip her, she is wobbly in the morning, careful, careful. Pack Lady is sad in the morning. I do not understand this. Morning is Happy Happy Time. Food Time.

Pack Lady looks for my Food Dish. I am a Clever Dog, I bring my Food Dish. Pack Lady says, 'Good dog.' I love Pack Lady, even in the morning.

'ERRO!' I say in ape-barking. Oh dear, Food Dish goes *kerlang crash* on Pack Lady's paw.

'Oh God,' says Pack Lady.

Yes yes YES. She has The Dish. OH JOY. She has a hard-shelled Food thing[1] in her paw. She is opening it with her clever paws. She is putting Butchers' Dog chunky food in my Food Dish. More MORE. Now mixer.

MORE MORE MORE.

---

[1] It is a mystery why apecats keep hunting hard-shelled foods which are difficult for Cats to open up. Some of the finest Feline minds in the world are working on this problem. One day soon We will solve it.

Oh OH quick QUICK. Pack Lady, I am
s-o-o-o-o HUNGRY.

Food Dish is on the floor. Hardest thing now.

Pack Lady says, 'Sit.'

I sit. Oh so hard.

Pack Lady says, 'Wait!'

I wait. Long long wait. Drool in mouth. Gug gug.
My TUMMY IS SO HUNGRY.

Pack Lady says,
'GOOD DOG EAT.'

YES! FOOD

FOOD SCRUNCH
SCRUNCH scrunch
slurp yum yum.

Erp.

Happy Dog. Thank you so much,

Pack Lady.

More?

Oh. Sorry.

All the Cats are there – Remy, Maisie and Muskie
going *Erow, mrow, yow, rrrp, rrryow*, which is cat-
talk for 'Feed me now, you stupid ape.' They
do not do respect for Pack Lady, except rubbing
their sides on her legs so she trips over them.

She opens a hard-shelled Food thing and puts it in the Cat Food Dish. It is very nice food (Kitekat meaty chunks, usually) and the Cats eat it up, very slowly.

I do not understand why Cats eat so slowly.[1]

---

[1] We eat fast enough, in fact, faster than We would like because otherwise the Big Stupid might eat up Our Food. It is iniquitous, in any case, that he has to be fed before Us.

SUGAR PUFFS!

Next Pack Lady goes upstairs again and lets the boy puppies out of their nest room. Down they come – clatter clatter bark yell push shove.

'I want Sugar Puffs.'

'CanIyava Free?'[1]

'Hi Jack. Here, look what I found under my bed – catch!'

Oh DELICIOUS – mature choccy digestive, SNAP, GULP.

'Pete, stop that. I've told you how important it is not to let Labradors get fat.'

---

[1] A Free is a little plastic toy for Cats to play with until the Big Stupid chews it up.

'Sorry, Mum.'

Pete's body says: *I love Jack, I will feed him anything I don't want to eat myself.*

He is my friend. What a lovely Packmember. Here is paws-up respect for you, Pete, I love you HUGE AMOUNTS.

'Ahhh, Jack. Good boy.'

And Mikey, you are my friend too. Yes, you can lie on my tummy and suck your thumb.

'Mikey, will you get off Jack and eat your cereal!'

'Where's the Free?'

'It's my turn.'

'NONONO, it MY turn, I wanta Free, Mum, Mum, canIyava Free . . . ?'

'Mum, it's my turn, you promised, you said . . . Ow!'

Push shove. OH NO. My Packmembers are hitting each other, they are fighting,

OH NO, OH WOW, ARF,

don't fight, fellow Packmembers, we are all friends here, oh no, what shall I do? I will interpose myself, oh wow please don't fight . . .

32

'THAT'S ENOUGH. You're upsetting Jack. Now, both of you, sit down and eat your breakfast or there will be NO TV tonight!'

Silence. Munch munch munch go my Packmembers, eating up their cereal. Pack Lady's body is still saying: *Scary, fierce, don't annoy me.* I hide under the table. It's a good place for me. Sometimes there is bacon hiding there, nobody wants it, slurp. Not today, though. Sad.

But while fierce Pack Lady is making the singed bread, Mikey gives me a fistful of nice Sugar Puffs and cow-milk from his bowl. Yum yum, slurp, lick. Delicious.

Pack Lady barks up the stairs for girl puppy. No answer.

Pack Lady opens the back door so I can go and do my Messages in the Outside.

NEVER
NEVER
INSIDE.

Outside . . . Trot round. Wet Message, Hard Message, Wet Message where a strange cat made his own smell (big tomcat, very fierce, ate Whiskas with beef and a Small Furry)[1] and scrape the ground to spread My Smell more, so it goes all over the Outside. Lots of grass and mud flies up behind me, shows I am a Strong Big Dog.

Sniff. SNIFF.

Nose tingling. Ears buzzing. Head goes whirly whirly.

There is a wonderful Smell.

A beautiful Smell.

Oh oh so delicious Girl Dog SMELL . . .

SHE IS READY!

PETRA IS READY!
OH OH OH WOW!
HAPPY DOG.

Yip yip YIP, says Petra in her Outside. *Quick quick, come and play the Dog&Bitch Game with me. Come on!*

But other barking. NotMyPack dogs barking. Lots of barking. They know Petra is Ready too. Oh dear. What if they want to play with Petra? Oh dear. What can I do? They sound very Fierce and Big and Strong. *Roof, roof,* they say, *we're coming, beautiful girl dog, we'll come and play, we are very Big and Strong, we*

---

[1] This is the orange—and—white enemy tomcat. We will kill him and eat him one day.

love you too . . . I can hear George and Fido III and Grrrr Garage Dog.

NO. Petra is MY friend.

 I say, ARROOOOF. It means Bad Things. I am saying, *I will bite you* to the NotMyPack dogs. I hope they believe me. I am scared. They sound very Big and Fierce. What if I have to fight?

Oh dear.

Maybe my Packleader will help with the other dogs. He is very Big. His bark is very deep. Maybe it will be OK.

Petra smell makes me feel better. I am STRONG. I am QUITE BIG.

I MUST GET TO PETRA QUICK.

I run to jump over the fence. Crunch. Missed. Oh dear. Try again. CRUNCH. Too high.

Maybe I can make the wood go away like a door. If you bash doors with your head, sometimes they go away. OK, let's try it. Back back, run run run CRASH. Not yet. Back back run run run CRASH. No. Back back run run run CRASH. Why is my head hurting?

More barking. They are very rude. I bark back.

ARROOOF. ARROOOF.

I say, *Bad Bad Bad, Petra is My Girl Dog.*

They say, *Bad Bad Bad, mine, mine.*

Lots of noise.

Pack Lady is here. 'What on earth is going on? What's all that noise, you bad dog?'

I am not a Bad Dog. They are. Often apedogs are amazingly stupid.[1]

Pack Lady gets my collar and drags me Inside, barking bad words.

Sad Dog.

---

[1] This is true.

ERRO PACKLEADER!

The girl puppy slumps into the Food room at last. She does not like mornings either. She groans as if she has a tummy ache. I say, *Hello, girl puppy* and she says the morning bark: 'Geroff you stupidog.'

Boy puppies stop fighting and yelling about breakfast. Now they are running around looking for removable furs and stuff. Creak creak, thud thud thud. Here comes Packleader! At last!

HAPPY HAPPY.

'ERRO, ERRO!' *Hi there, Packleader, respect, respect, how lovely to see you, I love you lots, where is My Food?*

'He's lying, I've fed him,' says Pack Lady.

Did she? When?

Packleader is not happy. He comes out of his nest room with only leg-coverings, scratching the fur on his belly and chest. Poor Packleader. So big and so little fur.

Hi, Packleader, what a lovely morning, hi, how are you? But he does not like it when I puppy-bounce. He goes in the room with the Big White Waterdish, then (oh sad) shuts the door before I can come too.

Why can't I come too? He is doing a lovely long Wet Message. Why will he not let me smell it? It must be a very wonderful Message, full of Bigness and Loudness. I love him SO MUCH. I wait for him, pant, pant.

'Coffee?' calls Pack Lady.

'Uh,' says Packleader.

'Jack was getting very excited in the garden and all the other dogs in the village were barking like maniacs. Do you think Petra could be in season?'

'Uuhhuur.'

'We'd better keep him in as much as we can. He was trying to headbutt his way through the fence.'

'God, that dog is dumb.'

Clatter, whoosh, squwish.[1] Out comes Pack-leader, nearly falls over me. Pant pant. I love my Packleader. He under-stands. He will help me to get to Petra and he will bite the other dogs and make them into meat.

'What's "in season"?' asks Pete. 'Is it about foot-ball?'

'It means, Petra's ready to mate,' says the girl puppy. Her body says: *Don't you know anything?* 'Mating is how dogs have sex.'

'When? Can I watch? When's Jack going to mate with Petra, Mum? Can I watch, can I? Can I?'

'Neeeowowow. Peeeow. I'm a Power Ranger! I killed you. Mum, what's sex?'

'Sex is how dogs make baby puppies, Mikey.'

'Oh. Why?'

'Er . . . so there are more dogs.'

'Oh. CanIyava puppy? Dackadackadacka peeow.'

'Cor, this is amazing. Will Jack really . . . ?'

---

[1] We do not understand why apecats use a thing with a nasty dangerous waterfull in it to do their business in. But they do.

'No. He's not going to mate with Petra. They're both pedigree dogs. Petra will be mated with another Samoyed dog if they want to breed from her.'

Pant, pant. Wag. I do not understand what Pack Lady is saying. What is 'mate'? What is 'breed'? When will she let me go and play the Dog&Bitch game with Petra?

'CanIyava puppy, Mum? Can I?'

'That's not fair for Jack,' says girl puppy, Terri. 'He's in love with her, why can't they just . . . ?'

'Because they can't. Have you got your homework? And why haven't you brushed your hair? Why do I have to keep after you for everything, Teresa? You can't expect to have a rat for a pet if I have to remind you about . . .'

Lots of noise. Lots of running about.

'Sorry, Jack,' says Packleader, slurping funny-smelling hot brown drink.[1]   Pack Lady has already drunk hers.

'CanIyava puppy, Mum? Dad, canIyava puppy. Mum, wanta puppy. Dad . . .'

Mikey has got his Food Box now, but he won't open it for me. Sad.

Pack Lady runs upstairs. Everybody runs. I run too. In circles. Rushing around, putting bits of

---

[1]   Coffee. Interesting smell. Poisonous.

removable fur on, finding paper and stuff. Much barking. Very exciting.

Pack Lady goes out hunting usually. She hunts lots of paper. I don't know why.

Pack Lady is ready now. Barking at puppies to get in the car, find homework, find crisps for break, where are your shoes? 'Ohforheavenssake, if you leave them out, you know Jack will chew them . . .' I jump around too. I am a Helpful Dog. They are all going to the Running Around Shouting House[1], even Mikey who goes to a little one.

They open the front door. Luscious warm smell of Petra comes through the door. My head goes whirly whirly.

YES YES YES.

I AM COMING, PETRA.

I'm running fast, soon soon we pla— Uurrrk.

Packleader caught my collar. Unkind Packleader.

---

[1] The apecats call this SCHOOL. It is a place to keep apekittens so they do not annoy Us.

Why can't I play the Dog&Bitch Game with Petra? Oh please.

'No, sorry, Jack,' says Packleader, still holding my collar.

Pack Lady and ape-puppies all run out the door, all barking.

JOY OH JOY: WALKIES!

First Packleader wanders round our den with his coffee, then paper comes through the little hole in the front door. Paper is fun. It makes interesting noises when you chew it and play tearing with paws, smells sort of treeish. But apedogs get cross if I do that. Why?

But today, before I can fetch and bring, Packleader runs and gets them. Oh great. GAME! Let's play chasing paper game. Yeah. Wow. I like that game, I can . . .

Oh. Sorry.

Some of them smell bad, so he leaves them. One he opens. He smells the paper for a while. Then he barks loud words. He barks like there is somebody he wants to fight. I jump up. ARRROOOOF! Where is the enemy? I will support my Packleader. He is very Big and Loud, it will probably be OK if I just follow him and bark a lot and maybe bite enemies that are already meat, maybe.

'OK, OK, Jack,' said Packleader. 'It's OK. We'll get 'em later.'

Funny day. My Packleader does not go to his little wooden den in the Outside to do smeary stuff. He marches around talking to the apedog talkbone with little apedogs inside,[1] and it goes psqueeeeoooo very high, makes my head feel funny. He stares at the clicky-clacky Flicker Box for ages, so boring, I go to sleep. HE FORGETS HIS LUNCH!

Then he makes piled-up-bread food[2] and gets old-milk-in-little-cups-with-fruit-in[3] and biscuits (yum, yes please, for me? Oh, sorry) and cow-milk-with-not-true-fruit-taste[4] in it and ape-food like

---

[1] Makes nice purring and squeaky noises, fun to play with.
[2] These occasionally contain Catfood such as ham and butter.
[3] Apecat kitten food, smells nice, funny taste. Cups are good for playing with.
[4] Yuk. Ruins nice milk.

bananas and apples[1] and stuff and puts it in bags.

Ohh. Wait. There is a sort of bubble in my head. I remember piled-up-bread food. It is nice to eat but also it means something important. What is it? Um...

OH YES!

SO EXCITING.

THIS MEANS WE ARE GOING EXTRA-SPECIAL GOOD WALKIES! WITH THE PACK! Yipyipyip yippee,

HOORAY,

OH WOW,

ARROOOF . . .

---

[1] Not really food at all.

'Down, Jack, quiet. Yes it's a walk, but later, just take it easy.'

Oh OK, Packleader, I will try and be good and patient and wait for you to fetch the puppies from the Running Around Shouting House. Bye bye, see you soon with the Pack.

Sigh. Boring. Nose between paws. Doze. Sigh.

Long long wait. Everywhere is Petra Smell. Sigh.

YES YES HOORAY. AROOF ARROOOF, WAG WAG. HERE THEY ARE, HERE ARE MY PACKMEMBERS, Oh much much bouncy.

HAPPY HAPPY DOG.

WALKIES. YES YES WALKIES. HERE IS MY LEAD, GREAT PACKLEADER, HERE YOU ARE . . .

AT LAST. OFF WE GO ON BIG HUGE WALKIES. OH SO WONDERFUL. HAPPY HAPPY HAPPY DOG!

First there is the boring hard road for cars, only a bit of interesting at the side where there are green things and leaves and old Messages . . .

GRRRR. Garage Dog left a Hard Message right on top of Mine and Petra's. It says, *I am a Big Strong [small] Dog and Very* FIERCE *and I eat Real Meat and I Kill Rats.*

I growl lots and scrape the hard stuff but it does not spray over to hide Bad Garage Dog's message. What a pity. I <u>HATE</u> HIM.

I leave a Wet Message on top of his, and Higher Up to show how he isn't as big as he thinks, but apart from that maybe Mine are not so impressively Fierce. I have never made anything into meat, except a Small Furry by accident when I sat on it.

I leave a Hard Message on a wall nearby, to show Garage Dog I can reach, but Packleader spots it and puts it in a bag. Why does he do that?[1]

At last we go down a not-hard path, interesting sandy mud, stones, pawprints from other dogs and lots and lots of Messages

... Suki, George, Hilda and Fido III have all been down in the last few days – so much news. Suki has dug up a bone, George has had a bad tum from eating a Very Small Furry, Hilda says Hi, and Fido III has been to the Bad Whitecoat apedog[2] for sharp claw sticking. It is very interesting.

---

[1]   Because, Stupid, apedogs know that it scares the game away, so they bury it in a bin. They are comparatively civilized, though having a waterfall in your litter tray goes Too Far.

[2]   Apecats call this evil creature 'the vet'.

Also lots from Small Fierce Brown Wild Dog[1] – dragging meat, some kind of Flying Feathery.

Also Small Fierce Stripy-Face Phew-Smell Dog.[2]

Also lots of small Furries and Medium Eatable Furries with Long Ears.[3]

---

[1] We think he means a fox. Worrying, but relatively civilized once you know them.

[2] Probably a badger. Very uncouth and occasionally chase Cats.

[3] Rabbits. Edible and a lot of fun. Scream loudly when you make them into meat.

Also Funny
Pricklies.[1]

So so exciting. Here Fierce Stripy-Face ate a
Prickly.[2]

Here the ginger-and-white tom made a rabbit
into meat and ate it. Yum. That was good hunting
for a cat. I have never known Remy, Maisie or
Muskie catch a rabbit.[3]

Long time since I was here, so I must leave lots of
Wet Messages.

My Packmembers are running about except
Mikey, who is riding on Packleader's shoulders.
This is so **GREAT.**

Now Packleader goes to some big nettles and
starts bashing them with a stick. Some rabbits and
Flying Featheries that were in there thinking they
were safe, suddenly run out. Woww!

---

[1] Hedgehogs. Not edible.
[2] Except by Badgers and cars.
[3] Obviously we could, we just don't choose to.

CRACK!

Oh. What happened? There were twinkly things all round me. Where is the rabbit?

Packleader is laughing at me, so are Pete and Mikey and Terri is stroking my head. There is a hole in the wall next to the path. It smells of Very Recent Rabbit. Oh. I think the rabbit went in the hole and I bashed my head on the wall. Sniff sniff! Yes, the rabbit is there, hot, frightened, hiding . . . YUM YUM. I dig dig dig.

No good. The hole is in the wall not the ground. Oh well. I don't know how to make a rabbit into meat anyway.

Behind the bashed-down nettles is a gate, very old and shut. Packleader tuts, opens it carefully so we can go through. Shuts it.

On the other side is a very old road, full of nettles and brambles. Underneath there are stones, though, like for all apedog roads. I sniff. Long long time ago, apedogs came here, Very Big Furries with hard paws came here, dogs came here, long long long time ago. So faint I can hardly smell it. Packleader has been here before, but not me.

Packleader walks down the old road slowly, bashing nettles out of his way with his stick. He is talking apedog barking to the ape-puppies. Snff snff snortle. Wonderful SMELLS.

There is another gate across the path. Next to it are steps in a wall – hup! scrabble scrabble . . . Jump. Splash, lovely puddle. Mikey likes it too. Why don't you want to splash, Terri? There is another path, small and very muddy. No dogs here either, more Wild Furries being very fierce.

Lots and lots of rabbits. Lots and lots. They smell so delicious. How do you do the making meat thing? Yum. If Cats can, why not Me?[1]

Packleader comes to a stream. Jumps over. Me too . . . whoops, splash. Never mind. Shake shake. Everybody barks the happy-morning bark: 'Geroff you stupidog.'

Oh. Wow. This is very strange and new. We are in an old apedog place. It still smells a very little of them, also of ground-up seeds. Ground-up seeds[2] is another kind of ape food, but dogs can't eat it, even after they have skinned it and the white dust-stuff goes all over the room – it makes you

[1] Because you're too Stupid.
[2] Definitely not Catfood.

51

sneeze lots. Also it is Bad Dog to skin ground-up seeds.

Anyway, this is a big stone and wood apedog place, full of wonderful other smells. Mushroomy smells, stone smells, Little Crawlies eating wood, old wood. I go smell in the den: quite dry, foxes were there, but not now; hard shiny stuff on the floor. Trot out again.

'OK, kids,' says Packleader seriously. 'This is a site of special scientific interest, it's practically untouched. There are some rare lichens and insects and flowers here. But it's not safe. Inside the old mill it's probably quite dangerous, and I don't want anybody going in there, especially as you might disturb some of the wildlife. There could be broken glass inside as well, carried in by flooding. You got that, Pete, Mikey? And stay away from the millpond

– it's got a dangerous undertow and it's full of weeds.'

Packleader has his box that makes lightning.[1] He puts it next to his face and makes it go click, whirr, click, whirr, but no lightning. My Packmembers are being extra-special good, wandering around, looking at things and dropping pebbles in water.

Packleader explores. There is a place outside where the stream is stopped so there is a pond – quite big. Full of Slimys and smooth WaterNotFurries, who live inside the water. Very interesting. I can smell them in the water smell, they are very different from Furries and apedogs and me, but definitely eatable.[2]

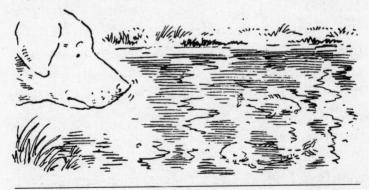

---

[1] Another kind of box that apecats go crazy about, this kind really does flash lightning. They say it makes pictures but inside is only long curly crackly stuff, with holes, good for playing with if you knock the box off a table so it breaks.

[2] He means fish. Fish are clearly Catfood, but hard to hunt because of the nasty water they live in.

Packleader is looking round the pond, looking at the green stuff. He stops still, watches hard. What is he looking at? I can't see it . . . sniff sniff . . . Oh. I smell it. A Flying Feathery, eats fish, male.

'Hey look at that, guys. A kingfisher.'

Where? I hear it fly away. Clever Packleader to smell it first.

Maybe the fish will be my friends. I sniff. Taste the water. Lovely interesting taste – bowl water is so flat and dull.

But Packleader gets my collar, we sit down.

'OK, people, teatime.'

OH DEAR: WATER-RUNNING

Packleader gives out the Food. Yes? For me? Tea for me, please? I like piled-up-bread food.

Oh. Sorry.

Everybody eats up. Pete gives me his crusts when Packleader isn't looking. YUM. I like peanut butter.

'Why are you taking photos, Dad?' asks Terri.

'For the *South Cornwall News*. The blasted motorway proposal is back again.'

'Some people think it would bring work to the area.' Terri has her I-am-a-grown-up voice.

'I wish that was true, but I don't think it is,' says Packleader seriously. 'Even with a motorway, Devon is still three hours closer to London and just as pretty. Meanwhile wildlife habitats like this will be wiped out.'

'Oh no.' Pete is sad. 'Why build one here then?'

'It's cheaper. And the cheapest route goes right through here. Right over the top. This would all be concreted over. That's why I'm taking photos for the paper. We're trying for a court order to stop demolition.'

'Huh. I'm a Power Ranger. I stop them, Dad. *Dackadacka . . .?*'

Terri looks cross. 'Here? All covered with motorway?'

'Yes. And the noise and fumes would be pretty bad where we live too. So we're trying to delay it and make it cost more than anyone wants to pay.'

Why is everybody except Mikey looking sad and worried? There are no enemies. Garage Dog is in his garage, fast asleep. We are quite safe.

Peanut butter makes my teeth feel itchy. I need a drink.

LAP, LAP, SLURP. Yum.

Hi, fish. Shall we play? Come on, fish. Jump . . .

56

SPLASH!

OH Oh DEAR.

Help. HELP.

No bottom to stand on. Weeds. Water-running, water-running, oh dear, it's hard. Help. Water pulling me under. Ohhhh . . . help

HELP.

Packleader is barking at me. His body says: *Angry, scared for Jack, must help.* All my Pack are barking and barking.

HELP HELP YES HELP. FRIGHTENED PUPPY. NO NO.

Water-running, quick quick to Packleader who is barking, barking lots.

'Nobody jump in, *nobody* – no, *not* you, Terri, it's too dangerous. I'm going to try getting him with my coat.'

Water pulling me down, weeds in the way, fish friends not helping. Oh dear, tired puppy . . . Why is Packleader taking his fur off?

HELP PACKLEADER. Water-running is hard because of water pulling me, weeds . . . OH OH. TIRED PUPPY.

Everybody yelling. Mikey is waawaawaaing. Terri is cuddling him. Pete is jumping up and down, yelping.

Packleader barks: 'Jack, *here!* Come here, boy!'

Water-run to Packleader, he will help, OH QUICK PACKLEADER.

Packleader kneels by the water, throws his removable fur on me . . . What? Why?

Again. Oh. I hold with teeth. Hold tight. He pulls his removable fur, pulls me towards him.

Packleader holds my collar in his clever paw. One two . . .

HEAVE!

Scrabble.

Oh. WHEW. Shake shake, Big Shake, splatter. *Thank you, Packleader, respect respect.*

Packleader is mad at me, he is barking his Big Deep Bark. My Packmembers are cuddling me and patting me. Pant pant. Happy Dog to have cuddles.

Packleader barks, 'You stupid great dog, you *idiot*! You're too thick to live.'[1]

Yes, Packleader, I am Thick. I am very Thick. Why are you mad?

'If you think I'm going in a slimy millpond to save a dumb dog like you, you're wrong.' His body says: *Yes I would.*[2]

Packleader loves me. I am his Junior Dog in the Pack. I love my Packleader. He is quite wet from splashes and grabbing my collar and when I shook myself. I lean against him, help to warm him up. Oh

[1] Evidently.
[2] Why?

dear. I left a big wet patch on his leg-coverings.

Mikey is still waaawaawaaing. I lick his face. He is tired. He wants his blankie. He has his thumb in his mouth. Lick his face again. Poor Mikey. Why are you sad?

Packleader packs everything up, all the nice bits in the bag to go home, lightning box on a string round his neck. Mikey rides on his shoulders again. Terri and Pete want to stay longer, but Packleader says no. He does a bit of snail-trail-stick scratching on paper.[1]

'Well, I hope that isn't the last time we see it,' he says.

---

[1] Cats are very interested in the intricate markings apecats like to make on white cat-bedding called paper. Feline primatologists suspect it may have something to do with apecat mating rituals. Or possibly, food.

SAD DOG, HAPPY DOG

Next day is not-school day. I am a bit Sad Dog because my Packleader is sick. He is coughing, *harroon harroon*, he is sniffing, *snorrk snorrk*, he is sneezing, *katchow!* He says it is My Fault.

He is in his nest, doing lots of puppy-whines so Pack Lady will feed him. She is not very nice to him. She did get him a funny yellow drink, smelling bitter like willow trees, but he didn't like the taste and put it in the upstairs Big White Waterdish. But she does not lick his face at all, she does not clean his paws for him, she does not even unswallow food for him.

Never mind. I am Packleader's Junior Dog. I will do these things for him, make him feel better. I will sneak upstairs (Bad Bad very Bad to go upstairs – but Packleader needs me). I will be very quiet very cunning get in Packleader's nest so he won't notice and cuddle up, make him feel comfy and not lonely. There. That's better. Poor Packleader.

Lick lick.

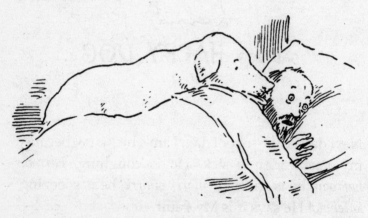

Oh. Sorry. Don't you like me cleaning your face? Couldn't we have a little cuddle?

Oh. OK. I promise no licking. OK. I love you, Packleader. Paws up. Rub tummy. ooooooh SO NICE rubbing tummy. I love you LOTS, Packleader. Rub more. oooooooh.

Ahhh. Sleep now.

'What is this big fat dog doing in our bed?'

Oh dear. Pack Lady is mad at me. Why doesn't she like it when I make the nest cosy and smelling nice?

Packleader does paws-up voice for Pack Lady. 'He only came to keep me company.'

Pack Lady sighs, goes downstairs. Maybe she has Food. I will go and see. I jump down, follow her.

'Traitor,' says Packleader and sneezes.

Pad round the Food Room after Pack Lady goes Outside, but there is no Food waiting to become Dog Food. All the Food is inside the Cold Cupboard and a box for hiding the bread and other cupboards. Very sad. I do not understand why my Pack keep burying all the Food in boxes and cupboards and stuff.

Terri girl-puppy comes to cuddle. She gives me some of her choccy bar. I save some for Petra. Happy Dog about choccy but Sad Dog about Petra.

Terri's body says: *Surprised! worried! something is wrong with Jack.* 'Do you think Jack's ill, Mum?' she asks the Pack Lady. 'Look, he hasn't eaten all of my Mars Bar.'

'No, he just wants to play with Petra, that's all.

And you shouldn't give him any Mars Bar, it's bad for him.'

Terri nods. Her body says: *Poor Jack*.

The boy puppies do not understand but they know I am sad. They all come for cuddle. They do quiet apedog-barking, hard to understand. Terri is saying how I am in love with Petra and they must help me. Yes, you must, yes please. Pete has a thing called an idea. They will do it. What is 'idea'? What is 'in love'?

Then when Pack Lady goes upstairs with some more hot drink for her Packleader, Terri gets my collar, we go to the back door. She lets me out, stays in the Food Room watching for Pack Lady. Pete and Mikey come into the Outside with me.

OH OH WOW. PETRA IS HERE. SHE IS IN HER OUTSIDE TOO!

Put paws on fence, *Hi, Petra, are you still Ready?*

Petra says, *Oh yes, yes, come and play!*

I try to climb over the fence. Oh dear.

Pete and Mikey look at the fence, they look at each other. Bodies say: *We are clever, we understand, we know what to do even if it's naughty.*

Pete goes and gets his box-with-metal-stuff. They go in the end corner, under the rhododendron. They put metal-things on a fence panel. It is loose.

Apedog puppies have very very clever paws. I watch, go sniff Petra, come back and watch.

Some fence has come off! I can get through! Happy Happy Happy.

OH OH WOW. OH OH WOW WOW.

Here is Petra! Lick face. Wag wag. Dance. Smell. Lick. Paws on back.

OHHH *@#'*^><****' WOW!

HAPPY DOG. I am a very very

HAPPY DOG!

Petra is Happy. I am Happy. So so Happy. Careful. Wait. Now. Joyful prancing. YES YES.

Pete and Mikey hiss for me to come quick. I come quite quick – no, Petra doesn't want to play any more. I squeeze back through the hole in the fence.

Very quiet, very clever, Pete and Mikey put the fence back where it was. They are very pleased. Their bodies say: *Wow*. They pat me lots.

Petra's Letitia is calling her back in.

Ape-puppies are so clever. I am Happy Happy Happy.

OH OH JOY! NOW FOOD TIME AGAIN. YES YES YES!

HUGE GREAT FOOD PLACE

Long long time later. Many many suppertimes, many many dark sleepy-times.

Petra's Letitia was talking to Pack Lady over the fence. They were complaining about Dogs and Food.

Pack Lady said I am the Greediest Dog she has ever met. This is Not Fair. I am Hungry. I am very Hungry all the time. When is Food Time?

Petra's Letitia said, 'Oh, you've no idea what a little pig Petra has turned into. She never used to steal food before but ever since we moved here,

67

she's been dreadful. She stole a
whole free-range chicken[1]
off the counter yesterday
and I only took my eyes off
it for a second.'

Clever Petra.

Me and Petra sniffed
noses through the fence.
She said to me, *My Pack Lady washes my blanket
EVERY OTHER DAY! How can I ever get it smelling nice
and comfy?*

Petra gets brushed and roaring-sucky-
tubed[2] every day. Bath two times a week. Ooh.
Scary. Even Petra's nice smell is very faint.

Poor Petra. She wants to be out in the Outside as
much as she can.

Petra's Letitia must be scared of smells. Scared of
dirt and mud and cow messages and good things;
likes pretend smells better. Why? Apedogs have
very strange noses.

But I know something special about Petra. First it
was just her Wet Messages. Then it was all her
smells telling me, even pawprints. Her smell says:
Look after me, guard me, feed me, I am Special.

I am not sure why Petra is Special but I will do
what her smell says.

---

[1] Very very delicious catfood. How slow and clumsy apecats
manage to bring down these huge birds so regularly is another
mystery Cats are investigating.

[2] Apes call this a vacuum cleaner. It is a horrible fierce monster
which might well eat Cats if We are not very careful indeed.
One day We will learn how to kill it.

Next thing in the back Outside when we are doing our goodnight Wet Messages, Petra puts her paws on the fence to talk to me. She tells me a Terrible Thing.

She says sadly: *My Pack Lady says no more treats. She says I am too fat.*

What is too fat? Petra is beautiful as well as Special. What is no more treats?

No choccy, no biscuits, only boring food.

Oh dear. Poor Petra. I must hunt her some food. But how?

I don't know. It's too hard for me. Then Muskie comes and sleeps on me. He is a Cat so he knows all about hunting. He tells me what to do.

So next time I see my Pack Lady getting ready for the Big Hunt,[1] I climb in the car when she's not looking, so I can go too.

---

[1] Those feline geniuses not working on the hard-shelled-food problem are studying the question of where apecats go on their Big Hunt. If only We could discover where the huge birds, shell-foods, fish and milks live, it would be a great advance for Catdom. Hence Muskie's important mission. There is a Shop near our lair but they are even stupider than most apecats and chased Us away when We were only investigating.

If I get in the back and lie down quietly, maybe she will not notice.

Oh. She did. But only a little bit Bad Dog: she thinks it's funny I was trying to hide. She says I can come if I am Good.

EXCITING. Where is the Big Hunt? WHERE IS ALL THE FOOD?

Cars have to drink horrible smelly stuff. First Pack Lady goes to get that. She stops in a bad-smelling place. Big not-trees with water-snakes, making clanking sloshy noises. I look out of the window, try not to breathe.

I feel like I want to unswallow breakfast, but that would be Bad Dog. Pack Lady sees me starting to unswallow, opens door, grabs collar.

BUT I DON'T WANT TO GET OUT. Garage Dog is very **fierce** and SCARY. He barks: *Rowf, rowf, you great big soft thicko, I'll eat you if you set a paw on my territory, gnash, growl.*

Oh Oh, SCARED puppy. What can I do? Bad Dog to unswallow in car. Dead Dog if I get out.

Whew. OK now. I unswallowed out of the door. Whew. That was close.

'You ought to be ashamed of yourself,' said Pack Lady, trying to wipe her paw-coverings. 'Great big dog like you scared of a little Jack Russell.'

Garage Dog is lying on the counter: *Yeah, I'm just the right height to* TEAR OUT YOUR TUM. *Wanna try me?*

He is a Bad Dog. After Pack Lady shuts the car door, so he can't get me, I tell him how Bad Bad Bad he is. Lots.

Off we go now. Fast fast. TREE TREE Tree Tree tree-treetreetretretre . . .

Wind on my nose, ears blowing. Wheeee!

Boring. I go to sleep.[1]

---

[1] This is a tragedy. The Big Stupid hasn't even bothered to learn Where It Is!

'Wake up, Jack!' My lead goes on. 'Out you come, Jack.'

OH OH. SO EXCITING. SMELL OF FOOD. LOTS AND LOTS AND LOTS OF FOOD. HUGE AMOUNTS OF FOOD.

Huge big den. Lots of apedogs. Shell-foods. Meat. Cakes. OH YUMMY. I will go to help my Pack Lady hunt. I will be a very good hunter in the Huge Great Food Place . . .

WHAT? Oh sad SAD puppy. I am tied up to a metal stick outside. I can smell SO MUCH FOOD but not eat. My tummy goes

GURGLE GLUB GURGLE

But not go in. Oh. Cruel unkind Pack Lady. SAD DOG.

Long long wait. I bark. Lie down. Can't sleep. Too much SMELL.

But HERE COMES PETRA. OH OH WOW WOW! Happy Dog. Petra's Letitia has to tie her up next to me because this is where the metal stick is, even though Petra's Letitia's scrawny body goes: *Yuk, scared, don't like you.*

I smell Petra. *Hello*, wag wag, pant. Happy Happy. *Please can we play . . . ?*

Snap. *No! Of course not.*

Oh. Sorry.

Petra does a nice little Wet Message, just for me. She is Special. Oh how Special. And very hungry. Poor poor Petra. Starving puppy. Letitia has put her on a Diet. What is Diet?[1] Letitia says she is too tubby.

Oh dear. *Never mind*, I say to Petra, *I will help*.

Lots of NotMyPack apedogs come past with food in their metal food-holders-on-wheels. I pant and wag. Maybe they will give me and Petra food.

No. Some of them pat and say, 'Good doggie.'

One ape-puppy understands and drops his sweetie for me, but it isn't proper food, it is that sticky chewy stuff, makes your teeth stick together, very hard to swallow. But I manage.

At last Pack Lady comes back. Oh oh JOY! She has been successful. I bark congratulations, I sing, *Clever clever Pack Lady, all on your own, without*

---

[1] An abomination.

your Pack, you have hunted a MAGNIFICENT MEAL for me and Petra, you are a wonderful Pack Lady! Clever and strong Pack Lady. Look at the shell creatures, bread, cakes and...

MEAT!

Pack Lady stops to talk to Petra's Letitia. There is a meat-thing on the top of the piled-high food-holder. It is that lovely pre-chewed cow-meat that tastes **WONDERFUL** until the apedogs spoil it by burning it on metal. After that it is only nice.

I am a Quiet Dog. Cunning hunter. Like Cats teach me how to help with getting Food.[1] Very very quiet. Pack Lady is patting Petra, who is doing paws-up for her.

Very quiet and soft, I take the lovely chewed-food packet in my teeth, lift it from the food pile, bite it open. OH SMELL!

YUMYUM.

Slurp slurp.

Erp.

---

[1] We are staggered and quite pleased that the Big Stupid remembered anything at all. We will redouble Our efforts to train him, despite the sorry failure of the Muskie Big Hunt project.

Oh. I meant to give it to Petra. She looks sad. I lie on the bits of food-skin so Pack Lady won't see. Letitia and my Pack Lady go off, put the Food in the car.

Petra smells me, licks my mouth like a puppy, goes yip yip. I know what she wants. Oh well. She is Special. She needs Food Badly.

I unswallow the food for Petra and she goes Yum, yum, slurp, slurp. *Thank you, Packleader, respect respect.*

Petra has called me her Packleader! OH OH WOW! I am PRRROUD.

I am a RRReal Dog. Nobody saw me, except some ape-puppies who think it's funny.

Petra's Letitia undoes her lead, she goes in the car still licking her chops. Yips goodbye to me.

Pack Lady comes and gets me. I jump up to tell her how I am Petra's Packleader.

Oh dear. She finds the food skins.

I am a Bad Dog. I am a Thief. I have had two pounds of mince. Oh dear.

She says, 'No supper, you Bad Dog.'

OH OHHH. I am SAD PUPPY. SAD DOG. Can't she tell I unswallowed it for Special Petra?

No. Apedogs are stupid that way. They only know what they can see.

75

Sad SAD SORROWFUL puppy.

In the car. Light-tree, light-tree. Tree tree tree-treetretre . . . never mind. I will be sad-dog-hungry-dog but I am . . .

Petra's Packleader.

PROUD DOG.

CHICKEN, PIZZA, MATURE STEW!

Packleader is acting funny. He has stopped doing smeary stuff in his little wooden den and is spending lots of time staring at the clicky clacky Flicker Box.

Sometimes more bits of paper come through the hole in the door. Packleader gets them and smells them and sometimes they make him angry: he marches up and down barking. I chewed one of them to show him I'm not scared of the paper Messages either, but that was Bad Dog because it was a Cheque. What is 'Cheque'?[1]

---

[1]   A kind of coloured paper that Cats must not sit on or put pawprints on.

One time a paper Message came and it made Packleader Happy Happy Ape. He waved it at Pack Lady. They have stopped a Bad Enemy apedog called Joe Bristol from demolishing the mill. They opened a bottle of Falling Over Juice.[1] I am Happy Dog too, but what is 'demolish'?

More days later.

Petra is outside in her Outside lots. Petra's Pack Lady doesn't want her waiting Inside when she and Petra's Packleader go hunting, because Petra is stealing too much food. She can open her Cold Cupboard by pawing it.

Petra is S-O CLEVER. She is the CLEVEREST Dog in the World.

But Petra is sad. She is hungry. She says her tummy is feeling very funny.

Petra says, *I don't want to stay in my Outside. I think my Pack Lady doesn't like me being Special. I want to find a nice cosy nest, nice and dry and private and safe. That's what I want. A nest for being Special in.*

I am Petra's Packleader. If she wants a nest for being Special in, then she must have it. But where?

I say, *My Packleader has a nice comfy nest, but he's in it because his cold is back. Would that be OK?*

No, says Petra, *no apedogs please – they are too clean.*

---

[1] Poison. Makes apecats act happy like Big Stupids.

78

I am offended. *My apedog Pack* isn't *too clean*, I tell Petra, *they have nice smells in their carpets even if their nests could be more interesting.*

Well, I want somewhere private, says Petra. *Nobody there at all. Not even you.*

This Specialness is very strange.

Also I am terribly hungry, says Petra. *Feed me, Packleader.*

But I am not clever like you, Petra, I don't know how to paw open the Cold Cupboard.[1]

Petra thinks hard. She runs round her Outside sniffing. Oh yes. There is a place in the fence that is not very strong. I remember now. That's how we did the Dog&Bitch Game. If Petra pushes it hard with her head, she can come through. Oh Clever Petra.

---

[1] Because We have only imperfect psychic control over our apecats We have not yet persuaded them to put catflaps in their Cold Cupboard doors so We can get in and eat Our Food whenever We wish. We are working on this oversight, however.

I sniff round. Where are my Pack? Oh, yes, Packleader is sick. Pack Lady is cross; in the front Outside she pushes the RRRRR-Thing[1] over the grass fiercely and it eats the grass for her. The ape-puppies are running around: Pete is hammering, Mikey is pretending to do the same as Pack Lady and Terri is lying in the sun.

OK, Petra, I think it's safe.

She pushes through the hole in the fence, into my Outside where I say, *Welcome, welcome, my beautiful Special Petra, please will you kindly do a nice Message for me?* She does a quick Wet Message to show respect for my territory. We go into the Food Room. There is our Cold Cupboard. She smells it.

Oh, Packleader, you have a lovely big Cold Cupboard. Lots and lots of Food in here.

Yes, I say, sad and proud. *Big and full, but how do you get in it?*

I will show you.

With her pretty little paw which makes such lovely-smelling pawprints, Petra paws and paws at the side of the Cold

---

¹ We think this is what the apecats call the Lawnmore, which makes the grass grow. It is the same species as the Inside vacuum cleaner, loud, nasty, dangerous and might eat Cats. When We know how to kill the vacuum cleaner, We will kill the Lawnmore too.

Cupboard. At last one of her claws catches on it and . . .

IT IS OPEN. THE COLD CUPBOARD IS OPEN. *RESPECT RESPECT, PETRA,* JOY OH JOY . . .

Shhh. Must be quiet and cunning like a Cat. *Yes, Petra, you are my Pack Lady and you are Special. Of course, you must choose first.*

A good choice. Chicken is delicious and a whole one with bones is even better.

What can I have? Err.

Hard choice. Yes, I will have the pre-chewed meat. I always like that. Yum yum slurprpp.

Erp.

Petra has finished her chicken. What next? Oh yummy . . . *Can I have some pizza too, Petra? . . . Thank you.*

CRUNCH CRUNCH.

Erp.

81

Ahh. Petra has found more meat. Bone with meat on. We have to take the shiny skin off first. I have one, Petra has the rest. Delicious. Lamb. Yum.

She is pawing again. OH CLEVER Petra. She has opened the little cupboards in the door where there is hard cow-milk fat, very nice and tasty and interesting.

We eat all of it. Ooops. Some cow-milk in a bottle fell over. Never mind, we will lick it. *Hi, Cats, come and join us. Would you like some milk?*[1]

This is FUN!

---

[1] We Cats would like to make it clear that We in no way insti-
gated this raid and only benefited slightly with some milk and
cream and a few packets of that very nice strong-smelling
pinky-red fish which would otherwise have been wasted.

Now, there is apefood in the bottom of the Cold Cupboard, not good to eat, leaves and fruit and stuff – my Packleader doesn't like it either. He always sighs when supper is made of it and says, 'That's food that food eats.' Sometimes he goes out and hunts a burger afterwards.

At the back is a very nice bowl of mature stew with a little fur on it, all the more tasty. I get it with my teeth . . .

Ooops... Slippery... SMASH!

Never mind. Slurp . . . Mmm. Interesting.

'WHAT THE BLAZES IS GOING ON IN HERE?'

Oh dear. Pack Lady has found us.

'YOU BAD DOGS, WHAT DO YOU THINK YOU'RE DOING, OOOOH, BAD BAD BAD!!'

Pack Lady is very mad at us for opening her Cold Cupboard. She is VERY very very mad. She has a horrid rolled-up newspaper in her hand. She is whacking, whacking. Cats all run away.[1] Petra yips and runs round the kitchen. I try and get between Pack Lady and Petra. Whack whack. Much much loud barking. PACK LADY GOING TO EAT US, OH DEAR.

Whoops. Pack Lady slips on all the spilled milk, falls over, still trying to whack.

Petra and me run out of the Food Room into the Hall.

Packleader is coming down the stairs, *cough cough*. 'What's going on?'

Pack Lady yells in the Food Room, 'Those blasted dogs have eaten EVERYTHING in the FRIDGE!'

Packleader tries to catch me, he is barking too. He sees Pack Lady rush out of Food Room waving her newspaper whacker, milk on her black leg-coverings and bits of pizza in her hair and he laughs so much he has to sit down. She is not laughing. She is barking and whacking.

---

[1] Not true. We felt it would be politer and more tactful to depart.

84

OH dear. Petra and me are running round the Hall, try and get away QUICK. Then Pete opens the front door from the front Outside to see what is happening. Me and Petra run over him, and out of the front Outside, jump over gate,

run

run

run,

Pack Lady will eat us, she is VERY FIERCE AND SCARY, QUICK QUICK RUN.

SPECIAL MESSAGES?

We run and run. Interesting smells. Very Big-Furry-with-hard-clip-clop-paws was here, male, young, eats grass, oats. NotMyPack apedog was sitting on him. Badgers. Foxes. Just in time I smell the path my Pack hunted down the other day. I take Petra there. She knows it too, though not all the way to the end.

There is a funny bubble in my head again, getting bigger and bigger. Pop! OH?

The bubble says: *What about the apedog place for Petra?*

This is very hard. I have to wrinkle up my between-ears face. Place for Petra?

Hey! Petra could have her nice nest in the old apedog place. It would be good. Lots and lots of rabbits for eating. Water for drinking. Warm and dry inside, mostly, and leaves and dry stuff for a nest.

Come on, Petra, I say, *I'll show you a lovely place to be Special in.*

Petra cannot run. She is too fat. Her tail-end is wobbly, her tummy is very very full. She does not want to unswallow and waste all that lovely food, but Packleader will come to find us soon. Must get away. *Come on, Petra, over the wall. We can walk.*

87

We trot quietly, like Fierce Wild Dogs, we are a Pack. Sniff sniff. Yum yum, lovely rabbits with long ears. I wonder how you catch them.[1]

It is easy to find the place – I just follow my own trail there. Here we are, sniff, sniff, snortle. There are some boring apedog things. A big piece of wood on a stick with paint smears on it. Some bright crinkly tape on sticks. Nothing else. It is nice and quiet and safe for Petra.

We go inside the place where the ground-up seeds smell is.

Petra waddles around sniffing. *Yes*, she says, *this is a nice comfy nest for me to be Special in. This is just right. You are a very clever Packleader, respect respect.*

I use my paws, push all the leaves and stuff over in the warmest driest corner. I go round a few times, make it flat. Petra pushes leaves too. It is nice and safe, a little place, all hidden.

Petra goes round in it lots. Then she whines and goes round the bigger part again. Lies down. Gets up again.

Oh dear. Is Petra sick? *I will lick you better, Petra, give you a nice cuddle.*

What? What is this? Petra is smelling very strange. She makes little puppy whines.

No, says Petra, *there is more Specialness happening*

---

[1] YOU don't, Stupid.

88

in my tummy. *Special kind of Message coming. You have to go away now.* Go away NOWWWW. *Or I* BITE!

Oh. Gosh. Whoof.

I'd better go away. Petra was looking very Fierce at me. Maybe she doesn't like me. Maybe all that chicken made her sick.

Try unswallowing, Petra? I say.

Noo. Grrrrowl. **Goooo.**

Oh. OK.

I go outside. Have a drink. Maybe Petra is sick. But she says not. What is a Special Message? She is whining. Oh dear. I must help her.

No, maybe not. She looked very Fierce then. Fur up, showed teeth and everything. Maybe safer outside.

Petra is not whining now. She is panting. Licking something. What?

OH OH ROWF. THERE IS A NEW SMELL IN WITH PETRA: WHAT IS IT?

I bark, *Are you all right, Petra? What is the new smell with you?*

Petra says fiercely, *I am very all right. I know what the Special Message is now, it is OK, but you MUST* go AWAY NOWW! Or I will have to MAKE YOU INTO MEAT.

Maybe she has made a rabbit into meat. Is that the smell? It has a sort of meatish tinge.

Rrrowf?

GRRRRR, says Petra. Go away or

I WILL EAT YOU!

How rude. Oh dear. Petra doesn't like me any more. I am not her Packleader any more. Sad sad dog.

I will go home. See how Packleader is. Maybe tell him about Petra being very strange and unfriendly.

NO SUPPER: ARROOO!

Hi there, Packleader! Are you better? Why are you out of your nest and walking along the path, going 'Phhheeeweeet!' between your teeth and also '*Harroon, harroon*, JACK! *Snork, snork* HERE PUPPY! *Urrr*.'? Are you looking for rabbits? You should be resting in your nest, getting better from your nasty cold.

Oh. That's nice, you were looking for me. Shall we go see Petra? She is very unfriendly, though. Can you smell her? There is Specialness happening in her tummy. It's all very strange. Oh. You've got my

Walkies lead. OK, Packleader, if it makes you happy for me to have my lead on.

Packleader puts my lead on. He is barking lots now, very quickly. He is saying Bad Bad. He is calling me strange names. What is 'vandal'? What is 'fiend'? Oh.

I think maybe Packleader is mad about something.

I wonder what?

I am a Bad Dog. Ever so BAD. Everybody is saying I am Bad. Bad Bad Bad. Packleader is barking angrily.

I do not understand. What did I do?[1]

PACK LADY IS <u>VERY</u> <u>VERY</u> <u>MAD</u> AT ME. I have done paws-up, shown tummy, but nothing calms her. She growls when she sees me and calls me bad names.

I am SAD SAD dog. Why is Pack Lady mad at me? Why is all my Pack barking at me?

Also I am very very Hungry and I know it is long past my suppertime. Maybe they are too busy being mad to remember important stuff.

---

[1] Nothing to do with us.

Here, Pack Lady, here is my Food Dish,
KERLANG
CRASH!
Now do you remember?

Pack Lady barks loudly: 'You're not getting any supper when you and your girlfriend have just emptied my fridge and trashed my kitchen, you greedy pig!'

What is she barking about? What is 'fridge'? What is 'trashed'?

My tummy is all empty, I am very VERY HUNGRY. Packleader, please help. Here is my Food Dish to help you remember.
KERLANG
BDOING!

'Sorry, big guy. She's right. You've got to remember, when you pull a serious big-time food raid, supper is definitely cancelled.'

What?

'Listen up, Jack. No food. No suppertime. Nada. Nix on the eats. Not the dog.'

WHAT? They can't mean it. It isn't true.
NO SUPPERTIME?

Oh. Oh sad saaaad puppy. AROOO! AROO! SUPPER IS CANCELLED! OHHH WOOO! SAD AND MISERABLE PUPPY. AROOOOOOOOOOOOOOO!

Pack Lady is waving a newspaper again. She looks dangerous. I go hide behind Packleader who is saying *snork snork harroon!*.

Prring, prrring. It's the talkbone barking. It means there is an apedog in it.

This time the apedog is Petra's Packleader, and he is barking lots. His voice says: *Oh dear, upset, cross and worried.*

My Packleader listens to Petra's John. 'No,' he says. 'Not since she broke into my fridge this afternoon . . . Yes, that's right. She broke into my fridge. Last I saw of her she was hightailing it over the fence with half a pizza and what was left of a roasting chicken in her jaws.'

Bark bark bark, goes Petra's John.

'Hasn't she turned up yet? That's odd. Jack's home again.' Packleader looks sternly at me. 'Where's your girlfriend, Jack?'

Does he mean Petra? Sorry, I've forgotten where she is.

'Well, John,' says Packleader, who doesn't really seem to expect me to tell him, 'all I can say is that if Jack knows where Petra is, he's not telling.'

94

More barking. Petra's Packleader is getting mad with my Packleader for not knowing where Petra is. Why doesn't he go out and sniff around himself? He'd soon find her trail, what with the nice pizza and chicken and stuff.

Packleader is getting cross too. His body is saying *You're an idiot* to Petra's John. I come and sit next to him and lean against his leg so he knows I am there to Back Him Up if he has to fight Petra's Packleader.

Petra's John is still barking, with a bit of a whine now. Packleader's body says: *Boy, what a jerk*. He barks, 'Well, maybe she's gone somewhere quiet to have her puppies.'

Petra's John barks more. He thinks my Packleader is crazy.

Packleader is trying not to get cross. 'Well, OK, I'm sorry if you didn't know your dog was having pups . . . Why didn't you take her to the vet if you thought she was too plump and eating too much? . . . No, I don't know who the father might be.' Packleader's body is saying: *Oh yes I do know who it is*. He is doing that big ape stare at me which makes me uncomfy. Have I done something Bad?

I don't think so.

14

BIG PIG-LEG: YUM!

All night I listen to my tummy rumble and try and do that thing with bubbles in my head. I have to get food for me and Petra. I am the Packleader. I must feed her. But *how*? I wrinkle my between-ears skin – maybe that will make bubbles with food-plans in them come.

Muskie the Cat comes and sleeps on my head. This is very helpful. Muskie is clever,[1] he helps me choose the best food-plan bubble while we hunt flying rabbits with our eyes closed.

In the morning I have a food-plan. It is a not-

---

[1] Actually Muskie is quite dim and a severe disappointment to his mother Maisie, but compared with the Big Stupid, of course, he's a genius. We will draw a tactful veil over the Big Hunt fiasco.

school day so Pete and Mikey wake up very early and get up and come running downstairs to watch the Flicker Box and eat cereal in the Flicker Box room. They are very nice to me, they know Suppertime was Cancelled.

'Poor Jack, you must be starving,' says Pete. 'Here, have some Rice Krispies.'

Pete is my friend. He gives me his bowl. Slurp scrunch scrunch. Erp.

A bit sneezy, but very nice. *Thank you, thank you, Pete, paws-up, respect, you are my friend.*

'That's OK, Jack.' He pats my tummy and puts more cereal and cow-milk in his bowl for him to have.

I bark to go out. In my back Outside I follow my own trail to the fence between my territory and Petra's. Push with my head, hard push, but careful, not too loud.

Now I am in Petra's territory, full of beautiful Petra smells. Sniff, snff, snortle. There is a little door in Petra's den door, like for the Cats in ours, only this one is big enough for Petra. Sometimes they lock it shut and then Petra has to stay Outside.

Today it is open so she can come back. I push through carefully, almost get stuck.

Inside, Petra's Food Room is very silvery like a Food Dish all over, clean and shiny. Nothing on the counter, nothing in the bin. Hardly any nice smells at all, except the ones coming from the Cold Cupboard. I sniff carefully. Petra's Pack are still in their nest, still asleep I think. They smell quiet and soft.

I think maybe I should be very very quiet and cunning.

I go to Petra's Cold Cupboard and paw, paw, paw.

YES! I AM THICK! I am also Very Clever. It worked! Oh clever ME.[1]

Inside is a wonderful thing: a big lump of MEAT! Huge. With bone. Perfect for Petra. Careful now. Food-plan bubble still there. I have to do this hard thing in my head, where I keep on thinking about Petra. Pig-leg. Oh YUMUMUM.

Ooops. Mustn't eat it all. Pick it up in mouth, careful, careful, no crashes. Drool drool. Smells so nice, tastes SO YUMMY. Oh this is very hard.

Quick. Apedogs may not be able to smell anything, but they can hear.

Put it through Petra's dog-flap, where Muskie has

---

[1] This new ability of the Big Stupid (clearly the result of his greater muscle and thicker claws) could revolutionize Cat lives.

a quick nibble at it. *That's OK, Muskie. You are quite small and this is a very big bit of pig.* I start pushing through the dog-flap.

'What the . . . ?'

Oh no, it's Petra's Letitia – OH WOW how funny! She has no fur on! She looks a bit like a chicken, only very skinny. Poor Petra's Letitia, she must be sick to be so skinny. Maybe that's why she needs a whole pig-leg to eat.

I bark, *Hi there, Petra's Pack Lady, respect, respect, I have just come to get this nice bit of meat which you were keeping for Petra because Petra is too Special to come and get it herself, bye now.*

Oh dear. Petra's Letitia is rushing up to grab my collar, only her body says, *Scared, frightened, don't know what to do.* Why? Who is she scared of? Maybe a big monster? Better get away quick.

Push through dog-door. Don't forget to pick up pig-leg in mouth. Oh DROOOL.

Push through hole in fence, push hard. Difficult with lovely food in mouth, yum, hard to keep thinking of Petra. Oh mmmff. But I am doing the hard thing in my head. I keep thinking of Petra's hungry smell.

I run through my den. Pete and Mikey see me. 'Hey Jack, where did you get that?'

I trot to the front door. *RRMMMF,* I say. Mouth is full of pig.

Mikey understands, moves to get the door open.

Prrring prring, barks the talkbone.

It's hard for Mikey because he's too little to reach the top part that lets the door open. Pete is going to help, but he's not sure he should.

Yes, you should, Pete, because you are my Pack member.

Prring prring.

Thud, thud, thud.

Packleader is coming downstairs.

Packleader stops when he sees me with my pig-leg. 'WHAT THE BLAZES . . . ?'

Oh dear. I think this is Bad Dog again. Quick, Pete, get the door open.

Whew, he does.

Prring prring.

Rush out the door just in time, over gate, run run, follow beautiful Petra smell, run run. Packleader gives up at the corner because his leg-coverings are slipping down and his paws are too soft without paw-coverings. He barks lots, though. Many many new types of word. I think maybe this is somehow Very Bad Dog. Never mind. I am Petra's Packleader.

When I get to the old apedog place – careful not to fall in the water – quick rrowf.

Hello, Petra, here I am. Here is a lovely present for you, only a little bit nibbled by Muskie who helped with the hard head stuff, and a bit more chewed when I forgot. Can I come into your den, it is nice and cosy, here is your food and . . .

OH WHUFFLE.

OH WOW!

There are little rat things next to Petra's tummy. Rats! They are eating her!

OH NO!

Petra lifts her head and her lip, *Stay away.*

Oh. OK. *What are rats doing there?*

Oh, hi, Packleader, it's you. Look what I've got.

Look at rats?

Smell them, silly.

Sniff, sniff, snortle, sniff. Hmm. Interesting.

OH! SO SURPRISING! Jump back. Is that right?

Don't get too close or I'll have to bite, warns Petra, curling her legs round the little squeaky wriggly things.

OHH. Her smell is different – fierce and . . . and . . . milky. Reminds me of Someone Very Nice a Long Time ago. Warm fur. Delicious milk taste in my mouth. Full tummy. A huge yellow Pack Lady licking my head. Very huge and warm. Love love love. Much cuddling. Oh beautiful smell.

The rats don't smell of rat. They smell of Petra and . . . and . . . something I know. A smell I know very well.

Snnnnfff.

ME! They smell of Petra and me!

OH WOW WOW! How exciting! They are not rats, they are dogs, they are very tiny dogs who smell of me and Petra. Their smell says: *Little, weak, look after us.*

This is what Petra was Special about. This is what Special means. Little dogs who smell of me and Petra.

Not for eating. NO NO NO! What are they?[1]

Puppies, says Petra, looking Very Proud. *I am a real bitch now.*

OH OH WOW! Petra has puppies. She is a proper Pack Lady at last! Petra is MY PACK LADY.

OH WOW WOW WOW!

SO EXCITING! I have to run outside, I run round and round the old apedog place, barking to tell all my friends.

Hey, Hilda, Fido III, George, Suki, Petra has puppies, pupuppies! I will help her feed them and look after them. If Bad Garage Dog comes near, I will
EAT HIM! I am now very Strong and Fierce because of my puppies and also my Pack Lady will help because there is nothing Fiercer than a Pack Lady defending her puppies so you better watch out, Garage Dog!

Rrrowf.

I go back inside. Petra lifts her lip again, just a little to warn me not to eat them. I would never eat them now I know they are puppies. They smell so pretty – half me, half Petra. Me and Petra, Petra and me. So Happy, so beautiful.

Petra is wagging her tail, thump thump. She says, *These are the most beautiful and clever puppies in the world.*

OH YES, PETRA, YES THEY ARE! WAG TAIL, WAG WAG WAG!

At the moment, though, they aren't doing much cleverness. They are squirming around and squeaking. Their eyes are shut. They smell of milk. I wonder if Petra would let me have some milk too, like my very nice huge Pack Lady from long ago. Better not to ask her yet.

Petra is eating up the pig-leg I brought her, and there's quite a lot of meat left on it. I was a good Packleader, despite awfully Hungry Tummy. *Can I share the bone, please, Petra? Thank you.* SCRUNCH!

NYAAAH! NYAAAH!

As I am the Packleader now, I go out to Mark my
New Territory. This apedog place is very very big.
It goes down the side of a hill. The bit where me and
Petra came in is a window and that is one floor.
Then there are some old steps going down (walk
carefully, they smell very bad and dangerous) and
there is another floor. This floor is all covered over
with mud and leaves and twigs and lots and lots of
shiny transparent glass things, lots of them, some all
pale and some dark colours. They are mixed up
with sticks and mud from the river. I leave some

Wet Messages on the wall, as high up as I can: *This den belongs to a very BIG, quite Fierce Dog.* Then there is another door, half covered with fallen-down wood. Outside there is a sandy bit that used to be a road and when I have marked it, I go along it.

What's this? A gate. Are there steps? Yes. Scrabble, scrabble, thump, splash. Oh, I know where I am. This is round the back of a farm.

OH WOW. LOOK.

They are a kind of meat. They are . . . sniff . . . White woolly meat? But alive. They go *Nyaaah, nyah, nyaaaaa* . . . They bunch up when they see me, they run to the other side of the field. One of them is looking at me fiercely – older female Woolly Friend. They go, *Nyaaaaaah.*

Oh, I remember. These are 'Keep Away Jack, No! No!' Woolly Friends. But no Packleader here to put my lead on and pull me away.

HI, FUNNY WOOLLY FRIENDS.[1] *Hello, how are you? Shall we be friends? Shall we play? Can I smell . . . ?*

Sorry. I didn't mean to scare you.

Why are they frightened of me? I only want to play.

Oh well. There is another gate, and I can squeeze through. More Wet Messages, it's another over-grown road, but some cars have come a short time ago. Trot trot trot, snnnff, snff.

Now I am back on the hard kind of road, trot trot trot, sniff sniff, leave a Hard Message. It's nice to be able to leave one that Packleader doesn't take away. He is so greedy about Hard Messages. He even picks up the ones I leave in my own Outside. Why can't he leave a few for other dogs?

It's nice going where I want round the village, not having to follow my Packleader or Pack Lady, not getting pulled away from interesting and delicious smells. Trot trot. Here is the shop. Snfff. There is a **LOT OF FOOD HERE.** Not as much as at the Huge Food Place, but a lot. Meat too. Interesting smells. Very delicious-smelling dust-bins. Oh yum.

---

[1] These are very interesting big woolly Food animals, that the apecats call sheep. They are edible, but only after apecats have killed them.

'JACK!'

It's Packleader calling. He is coming near.

OH JOY, I'M COMING, PACKLEADER. Run Run Run. Follow the wonderful Big Loud smell of my Packleader. Such a long time since I smelled him.

HI, PACKLEADER, HOW LOVELY TO SMELL YOU, HI THERE. I AM A PACKLEADER TOO NOW, PETRA HAS PUPPIES, THERE WERE WOOLLY FRIENDS . . .

Oh. Packleader is mad at me. He lunges at me and gets my collar before I can run away. He doesn't whack, he puts my lead on, he is taking me back to the den, he is barking at me. His body says: *Mad at Jack, seriously very very mad indeed.*

Why? What did I do?

I am a Bad Dog, but I do not know why. They say Bad Dog and shout about a 'whole leg of pork', but I didn't steal it, it was Petra's first. And I gave it to Petra. But they do not understand.

I go paws-up, show tummy, but my tummy is not magic today, he does not pat, does not rub.

Oh dear. Sad Dog.

I have made Pack Lady very cross. Also another NotMyPack apedog was in the talkbone and he said a big yellow Labrador was worrying his sheep.

Packleader looks in my mouth, then says to the apedog in the talkbone, 'There's no trace of wool or blood in his mouth, so I don't think it could be Jack. He's more likely to run away from them, I'd say, but I appreciate your concern. I'll make sure he doesn't get out again.'

The apedog barks, 'If that yellow dog comes on my land again, I'll shoot him.'

Packleader's body says: *Shoot you back if you hurt my dog*. But he says, 'Well, I know you have that right, sir, but I really don't think it was Jack.'

It's amazing how apedogs can say one thing in their bodies and another thing in their bark.

Also, what is 'shoot'?

Terri comes and cuddles me, 'He can't do that, can he, Dad?'

'I'm afraid he can, honey. Farmers have the right to shoot a dog that's attacking their sheep. Trouble is, dogs were originally wolves and sheep were originally what they ate. Once a dog gets a taste for chasing sheep, he never loses it and he can do an awful lot of damage. He doesn't even have to bite them, he can just stampede them and they'll injure themselves trying to get away.'

Terri wraps her arms round my neck. 'Jack would never do that.'

'I hope not. But we have to make sure he doesn't go off on his own any more. We have to make sure we keep him in all the time he's not being walked. You understand, Mikey? Don't open the door for Jack.'

'Neeeow. Peeeow. Megatron maximize!'

'You listening, Mike? No opening doors. Or Jack might get hurt.'

'Oh. OK, Dad.'

Now Petra's John has come round. His body says: *Worried, sad.* He talks to my Packleader about Petra. He still can't find her.

He is not a good Packleader for Petra. He didn't give her food. He didn't give her a nice nest for her puppies. I did those things. I am her Packleader now. If I was the Garage Dog I would bite him. I say so, not too loud.

Everybody looks. 'Jack!' says Pack Lady. 'What was that?'

'I'd lie low if I was you, buddy,' says my Packleader, growl in his voice. I make small, little puppy dog, lie down, show tummy. Nobody pats.

I am in Disgrace.

'I'm really worried about her,' says Petra's John. 'Letitia says she's probably been run over and good riddance.'

PETRA'S LETITIA HOPED A CAR WOULD EAT HER?

'Seems a bit harsh.'

'Well, Letitia's never really liked dogs, you know. She says they drop hair everywhere and make messes. She doesn't like cats either.'[1]

PETRA'S LETITIA DOESN'T LIKE DOGS????

---

[1] It is an unfortunate fact that some apecats are foolish enough not to like Cats. We do our best to show how beautiful We are, sit on their laps specially and so on, to demonstrate the pleasantness of Our warmth, but they remain foolish. Evidently these apes are even stupider than the normal run of apecats.

YUM! YUM! OFFAL!

I have jumped over both front paws Food times and a sleep, because the Cats said I should.[1] Also it was a Sad Time. I could not get Mikey to let me out to go see Petra. I could not paw open the Cold Cupboard. That's because my Packleader got a special little hook and stuck it on the door so it won't open. This is very very Sad.[2] I asked him to take it off, but he wouldn't, he just laughed.

I can smell on the wind that Petra is lonely and hungry a bit, though not very sad because the puppies make her happy. The puppies are not

---

[1] Aren't you glad We know how to tell a story properly?

[2] Not Just Sad. A tragedy.

hungry, they have Petra's milk. I bark to her, say I am here, I can't come now, my Pack won't let me out. I think she heard me, but it was Bad Dog for barking.

But how can I go to her when my Packleader won't let me out of the den?

Sad Dog.

Then Terri and Pete beg to take me for Walkies.

YES YES PLEASE, WALKIES!

They are going to get bread from the shop. Terri puts my choke chain on. Pack Lady tells her, 'Don't let him off even for a minute, Terri, he might get into trouble again.'

Sad Dog. How can I go and see my Pack Lady and my puppies?

Terri and Pete are tying me up outside the Shop full of interesting smells. Faintly on the wind, I can smell Petra. She is hungry and lonely. Oh dear.

An old apedog Pack Lady pats me. She is nice. Food? No.

I smell the metal stick where my lead goes. If I had clever paws I could undo it. But I don't. My claws do no good. I try chewing my lead. No good. It isn't chewable.

Sad Dog. But the Something Funny is happening in my head again, the bubbles coming up. Oh oh. It makes my head feel so tight. Inside the bubble is something to do with my lead. Something that happened by accident once. I shake my head, try and make out the bubble's smell.

My choke chain goes rattle chink. Oh. The bubble is getting bigger. I shake again. Rattle rattle chink.

Oh? OH WOW? I know. The bubble has just popped and I could smell it. Shake head, shake body, shake tail, shake head.

YES YES YES! My choke chain is getting looser and looser. Shake again. YES! AROOOF! It's off! It's on the ground! I can go anywhere I like, I am a very very Thick Dog and also Clever.

RROWF. I AM CLEVER. AROOOF, ROWF, BET YOU CAN'T DO THAT, GARAGE DOG!

Whoops. Muskie says[1] that when you are doing something apedogs don't like, you must be very quiet. Definitely no barking, no matter how excited your tummy might be.

OK. I can be quiet like a Cat.[2] Pad pad pad. Round the back of the shop are many lovely smells. I wonder if I can find something for Petra. There is a lorry there, with very cold air coming out. Inside are huge pieces of meat hanging up but too high to reach. There are boxes. The boxes smell very delicious, if a bit cold. Can I get one with my teeth?

---

[1] We are amazed and delighted that the most Junior Cat in our Pride has had such a benign influence on the Big Stupid.

[2] Not likely.

YES! OK, take the box in the bushes and skin it. Inside is lots of WONDERFUL DELICIOUS LIVER AND KIDNEYS AND HEART OH OH OH WOW WOW OWOOWF.

Yum. Slurp. Delicious and juicy. Oops. Mustn't forget I am hunting for Petra.

Get it in my teeth. Drag, carry like a puppy. Yes, it's heavy but I can do that. Off I go to find Petra.

Hurry hurry. The bag is heavy. I must get it to Petra before I forget and eat it all up. Oh drool. This is as hard as the pig-leg.

Carry carry pad pad pad. Here is the path. Carry carry pad pad pad. Smells of Wild Furries and things. Huge smells of LIVER and KIDNEYS and HEART. Pad pad. Drool drool. Put it down, rest.

Here is the gate, up over the wall. Through the nettles. Another gate. Whoosh. Over the stream. Wet paws. Careful round the pond. Can't smell anything except LIVER.

Just outside Petra's den I put down the food, give a little warning bark so she isn't frightened. *Rroof?*

Yes, says Petra, *you can come in, Packleader.*

Proud, so proud to be Petra's Packleader.

Look, my Pack Lady, look what I hunted for you. Isn't it lovely?

Oh yes yes YES, *my Packleader.* HOW WONDERFUL, *you are so clever, such a good hunter, congratulations, all by yourself you have hunted me a splendid meal! Thank you, thank you, much respect.*

Petra skins the meat and eats it all up. I watch her eat. It is nice to see how she gulps and snaps and licks the blood off her pretty nose. I lick out the inside of the skin when she is full. Yum.

The puppies squirm next to her tummy and go squeak, glug, squeak, glug. I wish I could have some of Petra's milk too, it smells delicious, but she won't let me. *You're not a puppy,* she says firmly. *You are my Packleader.*

Yes, I say. *Is everything OK, Petra?*

Well, says Petra, *not quite. There were NotMyPack apedogs here last night, and they smelled dangerous. They were all fierce large mature male apedogs, they did lots of barking and smelling papers and eating smoky sticks. They had hard things on their heads and big boots. They came in cars with big wheels. I thought this was a safe den but I might have to move the puppies.*

Oh gosh. This is **SCARY**.

I go out, sniff sniff snortle. Petra is right. **GRRRR.** One did a Wet Message on the wall downstairs. **GRRRRRRR!** It says:

116

Large, mature, male apedog, ate steak, chips, beans, chocolate and drank fizzy Falling Over Juice that smells of bitter herbs, burnt rotten grass seeds and yeast, not very healthy but extremely Fierce and Strong.

GRRROWF!

I do a Wet Message right on top, and a Hard Message, show him whose den this is. How dare he mark where Petra has her puppies? I will make him into meat and EAT HIM,

grrrr.

Petra says: *You are Fierce and Strong and Big, my Packleader.*

I hope this is true.

Outside on the sandy bit are the pawprints of two cars, with the car-blood smell. The apedogs stood around here. They have changed something, they have opened the gate. What is happening?

Yes, Petra is right, this is very bad. We must move the puppies.

I go back inside. The puppies are asleep. Petra is dozing off because her tummy is full.

Hi there, my Pack Lady, I say. *You are right about the NotMyPack apedogs. They are all over the place. I think we should move the puppies soon. The smells are making my fur stand up.*

Mine too, says Petra. *But where shall we take the*

puppies? They must go somewhere warm and quiet and safe.

All right, my Pack Lady. I lick her head between the ears. *It will be OK, I will go and find a nice safe place for the puppies.*

I know you will, says Petra sleepily. *You are so Clever and Strong and Brave, much respect.*

Oh dear.

PIG'S EAR!

I will go and look. Trot trot trot trot, down the creaky bad-smelling stairs, trot out through the door, trot through where the NotMyPack apedogs have made bad smells and danger for Petra . . . grrrrrr . . . Out the gate, down the lane, across the field.

Hello, woolly friends. Want to play?

Oh. Sorry.

Here is the boring hard road to the village. Trot trot trot.

Here comes a big male apedog. Who is it? Sniff. Sniff . . .

JOY. OH JOY! HI THERE, PACKLEADER, HOW LOVELY TO MEET YOU, SHALL WE GO FOR WALKIES AND FIND PETRA A BETTER PLACE FOR HER PUPPIES? . . . HAPPY HAPPY TO SMELL YOU . . .

Oh dear. I can smell that Packleader is mad. His body says: *Very very mad at Jack, but trying not to show it.*

Oh dear. What can I do? Stop first of all. Do the hard head stuff. Should I go to Packleader?

No. He's coming towards me, stretching his clever paw for my collar. Whoops, quick dodge, run backwards.

Oh gosh gosh. Packleader is chasing me, where can I go,

quick
quick
run
run
run . . .

Over the wall, down the ditch, run fast through the bushes, he is making loud crashing noises behind me and barking 'Bad dog!' It is so sad to disobey my Packleader on purpose but I am Petra's

Packleader now and I must find her a better den. Then I will go to Packleader and do paws-up, show tummy. Maybe he will not eat me.

Run
run
run,
very
very
fast.

Packleader can't keep up, especially through thick bushes and brambles because he is too big and the brambles catch his removable furs and make holes in them. He is roaring and growling now. Oh dear oh dear, if he catches me it will be much whacking and even more Loudness, ooooh, scary Packleader ... Run
run.

Whew. He has stopped now.

Pad pad pad. Trot trot. Sniff the wind.

Vrroom, car goes by. Cars can be very fierce and dangerous.

Oh yum. Here is a nice horse Hard Message, specially for me. Sniff sniff snuff, snortle, slurp, chomp. Delicious, full of maturity and complex fermented grass taste. What a wonderful Hard Message. I will roll in it to hide my own smell –

that will confuse my Packleader.

Vrrooom. Here comes another car. Oh, it's slowing down. I know this car. It is Packleader's car. AND MY PACKLEADER IS IN IT! OH JOY OH HAPPY HAPPY HAPPY! CAN WE GO FOR A DRIVE, PACKLEADER, CAN WE CAN WE?

Packleader has stopped his car and he is climbing out.

OH OH WOW. HE HAS A BISCUIT. HE IS SHOWING ME A LOVELY DELICIOUS CRUNCHY BISCUIT, THE KIND WITH BLOOD MIXED IN. IT IS VERY DELICIOUS AND . . .

But the head bubble thing is happening again. It says: *If you eat the biscuit, Packleader will put your lead on, the lead he is hiding in his leg-coverings.* His body says: *Careful now, cunning, catch the dog.*

He is saying, 'Here, Jack, here boy, good dog.'

Oh dear. It is so sad to disobey Packleader. But Petra has puppies. Packleader is very important but Petra is more important.

So sorry, Packleader, respect. I can't have your so-lovely biscuit present. Bye. Sorry. Oh gosh, he's running after me again, oh dear oh dear.

Jump through the hedge, run in the field full of big grass with seeds on. Packleader crunches through the hedge, saying bad words. But he can't catch me, I am too fast and also small enough to get through bushy bits. ARROOF. *RESPECT, RESPECT, PACKLEADER, BUT PETRA NEEDS ME MORE.*

Out on the other side of the field, onto another hard boring road. There are lots of hard roads and lots of soft roads round here. There is a den that has apedogs who go away most of the time and then come back sometimes. They have gone now, there are no plastic toys on the grass. I will have a sniff round.

Snff snff. Snortle. Mmm. All the smells are old and stale. Nobody here for a long time. The car-den door is a little bit up. Push with head.

Here is the car-den inside. It smells a bit of old car-blood, but not too bad because they do not ever put their car in it. There is a huge Cold Cupboard, there is wood, there are toys, there are bags with old ape removable furs in. Hmm.

Maybe this would be good. I go outside and leave

a Wet Message: *This is my den now, by a very Big Fierce Packleader (Me), who recently rolled in horse Message.*

Now I must go back and find Petra. Sniff sniff. No smell of Packleader, except a long way away in his car.

OH SMELL! Pack Lady is walking with the ape-puppies. Maybe they are hunting. I will say hello.

Hi, Pack Lady, how are you, how are you, Packmembers, Petra has . . .

Oh, whoops. Pack Lady's body says: *Careful, careful, cunning, do not let Jack see the new lead I've got for him.*

Terri has the sore eyes and smeary face from the thing apedogs do when they howl, making water in their eyes. Why is she so sad?

All the ape-puppies' bodies say: *Pleased to see you, Jack, careful, careful, we have to catch you!* 'Here, Jack,' they say, 'come here.'

'Cor phew, Mum, Jack rolled in horse poo again, whew . . .'

Oh wow. Pack Lady has a lovely biscuit with chicken in it. OH WOW WOW WOW. Terri has a pig's ear, she is showing me. I love pigs' ears. YUM YUM.

I run in, very quick, very careful. Pack Lady tries

to catch my collar, I knock the biscuit out of her hand, crunch crunch, dodge Pete, Pack Lady has my collar, pull away quick! Her clever paws aren't as strong as Packleader's. Whew, knock pig's ear out of Terri's hand, catch, hold in mouth OH DROOL but must take it to Petra . . .

Run away quick through bushes. My Pack are all barking at me, Pack Lady is saying bad words too. Everybody smells very mad at me.

Oh dear. Never mind. I will take Petra this lovely pig's ear, it will be entertaining and soothing for her to chew it when she is alone with her puppies. Even better than sticks because of the nice taste and no splinters.
Trot
    trot
        pad
            pad.

Must be careful. I can smell my Packleader's car coming. I will hide in the bushes, lie down like a Cat. Very quiet. Vroom. Oh NO, it's stopping.

It stops where I went in the bushes. All my Pack are out of the car, standing by the side of the road, all talking at once:

'Yeah, Dad, he went right through the bushes, there . . . See, where they're broken.'

'Neeeow peeeow. I'm a Power Ranger.'

'Shut up, Mikey. This is serious.'

'I not listening to you, Terri, you're just a girl.'

'No, but Mum, didn't you see what he did? First he got the biscuit from you and crunched it up and then grabbed the pig's ear off me, but he didn't eat it.'

'I'm sorry,' says my Packleader. 'Did I just hear you say Jack didn't instantly guzzle up a pig's ear?'

'Yes. That's why I let him take it . . .'

'You didn't let him take it, he bounced it out of your hand, didn't he, Mum, Terri didn't let Jack . . .'

'Shut up, Pete, and let me finish.'

'Well, you're not saying what happened . . .'

'Neeeowwwww . . . Jack is a Power Ranger Dog. Dogatron, maximize.'

'Shut up, Mikey.'

'No. You shut up.'

'EVERYBODY SHUT UP.'

Silence. My Packleader has the Loudest Bark in the World.

'OK, Terri, you talk first. What were you saying about the pig's ear?'

'Well, you see, I thought if he got the pig's ear he'd lie down nearby and chew it like he always does and then he'd be distracted and then we could all catch him.'

'Yeah. I see your thinking. That's good.'

'But it didn't work because he carried it in his mouth and just ran away. Like he was taking it to someone.'

'Uhuh.'

My Pack Lady barked next: she had the sound in her voice like apedogs do when they are Thinking which is an apedog thing which I do not understand. 'Tom, that's what the butcher said too. He said Jack got two of the bags of offal, but there was only one empty bag. He must have dragged one away with him.'

'Hmm. Petra hasn't turned up yet, has she?'

'Exactly.'

'What? What is it, Dad?'

'Well, maybe Petra's got puppies.'

'Gosh!'

'Yes, and Jack's helping her look after them. Wolves do that in the wild, don't they? The dog wolf goes hunting for the bitch, doesn't he?'

'Yeah, Terri, that's right, they do that.'

'Of course.' Terri has a happy sound in her voice again. 'Oh, that would be just like Jack. He'd make a great dad.'

'OK, we can't stand here talking, we've got to find Jack and Petra. And that's a bit more tricky, because a bitch with puppies can be very dangerous. Even Petra might bite you if she thinks you're a danger to her pups.'

'CanIyava puppy, Dad, can I?'

'So even if you find their den by accident, don't go in – you must come and get me, OK?'

Oh, wow. It is so hard to just lie here and not say, *Hi, how are you, my Pack, lovely to see you.* It's hard and lonely to lie in the bushes and smell their lovely friendly smells and hear their barks and not go to them.

I must do it for Petra because I am her Packleader. I can do it for Petra and the puppies.

RABBIT! RABBIT!

Here is Petra's den. Are there any NotMyPack apedogs around? No, good, just the old smells, now covered up with my nice new ones and Petra's too. Petra has done a Wet Message for the apedogs too, next to mine. Sniff snortle. Whew, chiff. What a fierce, strong, motherish Message! Surely even apedogs will be scared by that: if I didn't know Petra, and I smelled the Wet Message saying, *Large, strong, very furry bitch, just ate lots of liver and kidneys, Very Fierce (because of puppies)*, I wouldn't dare go near.

But Petra is my Pack Lady, so I am only a little bit careful.

Hi, my Pack Lady, respect, how are you, how are the puppies, I have found a good den, we can go now, if you like.

Hi, my Packleader, says Petra. *Puppies are all asleep and I am not comfy carrying them about in daytime. We will move them when it gets dark. Is it a long way?*

Yes, I say, showing with my nose. *Sort of that way.*

Oh good, says Petra. *I want to be a long way away from the NotMyPack apedogs who smell so unfriendly. Have you got me anything to eat?*

Er . . .

Oh dear. I remember now. I had a pig's ear to give to Petra, but I ate it by mistake when I was hiding in the bushes from my Pack. Whoops. It's lucky they didn't smell the lovely pig's-ear smell and come and find me.

Well, I did have something, Petra, but I'm sorry, I ate it.

Petra sniffs my face. *I'm hungry again. Please go and hunt me some food. There are plenty of fat young rabbits around here. I would like one of them, please, great Packleader.*

Er . . .

But I don't know how to . . .

Oh dear.

Pad pad trot trot. Sniff snortle sniff snortle sniff snortle . . . Whew chiffff. Lots and lots of rabbits here. Old ones, young ones, motherish ones. Lots and lots and lots and lots. But they are hiding in their holes. Dig dig. No, too hard.

Pad pad. Yowp! Look, a slimy leaping thing. Can I catch it, can I . . . ?

Whoops! Nearly fell in the millpond. That's dangerous. Not sure why, but it is.

Maybe I could catch a Flying Feathery. How do Cats do that? Walk very quietly, very quietly, creep up and . . .

Rowf rowf AROOOF AROOF ARROOOF!¹

---

¹ It's sad really.

Oh. They flew away. How do they do that?

Pad pad. Snff. Lie down where there is lots of smell of rabbit. This is very hard. I don't know how to do this Hunting Furries stuff. The Cats know. They do it lots. Some Furries can be fierce. Once Terri had a kind of small fat Furry and when I put my nose in its den to smell its funny smell and see if it wanted to be friends, it BIT MY NOSE.

It was very scary. I ran away. The Furry made chitter chitter squerrrk noises and stood on its back legs and showed its nasty sharp yellow teeth. I hid behind Packleader and everybody laughed. Packleader said what did I think I was, letting a hamster see me off.

But it was a fierce hamster and it had Big Fierce teeth. It did Fierce Wet Messages too, saying: *Fierce small female Furry, likes to eat apples and seeds, BITE YOU IF YOU TRY TO EAT ME!*

But I can't tell Petra I am scared of Furries, she will think I am not so great a Packleader and that would be bad.

Maybe the rabbits aren't as fierce as hamsters.

They are bigger, though.

Oh dear.

Smell. A young male rabbit is hopping slowly down the path. Now why can't he smell me? Oh yes, wind moving from him to me, also the horse Message fragrance is helping. Right. Now what do I do?[1]

He is eating grass, nibble nibble nibble. Gosh, what big yellow teeth. Like the hamster's, only bigger. Maybe he is too scary.

He smells very delicious, though. Very very foodish. There is drool in my mouth. Stay still. Here he comes.

Jump at him, he hops off, chase chase, run run. Rabbit is diving in and out of bushes, run run, he is scared, I can smell he is scared . . . Oh wow wowwow, this is fun, this is exciting, **run run...**

---

[1] Stay still, you blithering nitwit.

BITE! CRUNCH! SHAKE SHAKE SHAKE! Blood on my teeth. Yum.

OH WOW. I AM RRRRREAL DOG. I AM A PRRRROPER DOG. I HAVE MADE THE RABBIT INTO MEAT![1]

RRROOOWW, ARRROOOOF, ROOOF.

I am a GREAT PACKLEADER. I have killed a rabbit with my teeth, he is meat now, I can eat him . . . Wait. I will take him for Petra. She will admire me, give me much respect.

Pick up the meat, carry it in my mouth, careful now not to drop it. It is getting later now. Soon it will start getting dark. Petra can eat my kill and then we will take the puppies to the new den.

Pad pad . . .

Stop. Freeze. I can hear Petra's alarm bark. She is angry and scared. She is making herself get Fierce for the puppies. I can hear her, all my fur is standing up.

Packleader, help, yelp roof, arroowf, help, apedog coming to get my puppies.

WHAT?

---

[1] Astounding! Truly amazing! Must have been a very stupid rabbit. All thanks to our training, of course.

Run
run
run.

Drop the rabbit. Run, jump through the door. I can see the apedog. Air going the wrong way, I can't smell him yet. He is standing on the stairs. He is big. Very big male apedog. He is slowly taking his removeable fur off.

Petra is at the top of the stairs, all her fur is up, she is huge and very dangerous, she has all her teeth showing.

GRRRR, GRRRR, GRRROOOFF, GRRRR

... You try and eat my puppies and I will KILL YOU!

Petra is very beautiful and very Fierce.

I am pretty Fierce too.

ARROOOOF! ARROOOF!

The apedog turns slowly and I smell him.

OH NO! IT IS MY PACKLEADER. I HAVE BEEN DISRESPECTFUL TO MY PACKLEADER!

Run up stairs, interpose myself between Petra and my Packleader. Don't fight, we are all friends here . . .

(very quiet crack)

What was that? Jump down again, smell the wood.

(another very quiet crack)

The bad-smelling stairs! They are cracking! *Quick, Packleader, jump down quick, the stairs are cracking . . .*

QUICK QUICK RUFF RUFF, QUICK!

He is still going slowly. He is backing down the stairs. OH QUICK . . . ARROOF!

CREEAK!
CRACK
CRACK
CRACK . . .
CRUNCH . . .

'Oh NO . . . arrrhgh!'

Crunch

clatter clatter...

THUD

(crack).

THUD...

Clatter clatter.

'Uhhhh.'

YOWCH!

OH NO! What happened? Where is my Packleader? Where are the stairs?

Petra barks down at the piles of wood and sticks. *Where did they come from?*

Nobody is coming towards her now. She unbristles her fur, goes back to her puppies.

I come and sniff the sticks. Where is my Packleader?

'Ohhh.'

I can smell him. He is under all this wood that has suddenly happened instead of stairs. OK,

Packleader, I can find you, I will help.

I think he is hurt. I can smell hurt and there is blood too.

Oh dear, Packleader is hurt. I MUST HELP.

Big lump of wood, drag drag drag. Another lump of wood. Drag. Another. And another. Dig dig dig. HERE HE IS. Oh JOY OH JOY OH JOY. *Hi, Packleader, how are you, are you OK?*

No. My Packleader is not OK. He smells bad. He has a scared smell and a hurt smell. There is blood on his head. I will lick it better. Lick lick. Poor Packleader. This will make you better. Lick lick. He is sleeping, I wonder why. His paws have blood too. I think there is a bad hurt on his leg, it smells hot and poorly, though no blood.

Lick all the blood off, make him nice and clean. Poor Packleader. I will keep you warm.

He blinks, wakes up. Tries to pat my head, then he makes a hurting gasp noise. 'What the . . . Jeez, Jack, what happened?'

Pant pant. *The stairs suddenly turned into wood and you fell, Packleader. Are you OK now?*

Petra has heard his voice. She comes out and stands where the stairs were. She is fur-up again and fierce and she barks at my Packleader.

My Packleader understands. 'OK, Petra, OK, I'm not going to hurt your puppies.'

My Packleader always has a nice *I-like-you* smell and his voice is comforting and deep and so Petra lets most of her fur down, except for her neck. She does a few more barks, and goes back to feed the puppies.

My Packleader smells hurting. I lick his leg where it smells bad and he makes a puppy yelp. Oh dear, this is terrible. My Packleader is badly wounded. What can I do?

'I guess there's no chance you could make like Lassie, huh, Jack? Go fetch somebody? Get help?'

I do not understand what he wants. Pant pant pant. Lick his face. Don't worry, Packleader, I will help you if I can. First we must get your face nice and clean and your paws. That's better now. I will look after you until your leg gets better.

Maybe he is hungry. Now I know I had some food here somewhere. Where is it?

Sniff sniff snortle. Smell of rabbit meat on me. Oh yes, that's it. I go outside to find the rabbit. There's a smell of cars somewhere, but not close. There is the rabbit, with a black Flying Feathery biting it.

No NONO! Run at him very fast, barking lots. Arroooff ROWF ROWF ROWF ROWF! This is MY RABBIT!

The Feathery flies off barking bad things about how he is hard and mean and he will get me later. I pick up the rabbit by the head, bring it in to where Packleader is still lying down with his leg bent funny. He has got wood all around, so he can't move.

Here you are, Packleader! Here is a lovely fat juicy rabbit WHICH I MADE INTO MEAT, ME MYSELF, ARROOOF, I AM A RRRRREAL DOG, LOOK THIS IS HOW, SHAKE SHAKE, here you are, you can have it.

I carry it to my poor Packleader and put it on his tummy so it's easy for him to eat.

He goes, 'Uuggh.' I do not think he likes it. His face is showing teeth. Oh, he is trying not to laugh.

'Well, thank you very much, Jack, but I don't feel hungry right now. Hey, did you catch this yourself? You didn't just sit on it? No, clearly not, well, that's very clever of you. Good dog.'

Pat pat my head. OHHHH LOVELY. I LOVE YOU, PACKLEADER. Lie down next to you, paws-up. Pat my tummy. OoooOOOOooh <u>SO</u> NICE.

HAPPY Happy Dog.

Petra is standing above. She has smelled the rabbit. *Is that my rabbit, O my Packleader?*

Yes, Petra, I say, *my Packleader says he is not hungry and you should have it, much respect from him and me.*

Bring it to me, says Petra.

I pick up the rabbit, jump over the wood by the door, round and up the side of the hill, in at the window. There is Petra, very very mothery, lots of little puppies squeak-glugging on her tummy. I lay down the rabbit for her and she pants, shows paws-up as much as she can for me.

Thank you, Packleader, respect. What are you going to do about the apedog downstairs?

He is MY *Packleader, respect, he is safe for your puppies, also he has a hurt leg.*

Oh. Yes, I remember his smell. He is friendly. Are you sure he is OK for my puppies?

Yes, my Pack Lady, I am sure. He is my Packleader, they are his puppies too.

Grrrr, says Petra, *just so long as he doesn't come near.*

I go to where the stairs were and almost fall over the side. It is very high up – no wonder Packleader got hurt falling down.

Packleader looks up at me. 'Here, Jack.'

OK, OK, coming, Packleader.

Petra is crunching up my rabbit, lovely smell of meat, makes me drool. Maybe she will leave me some.

I go round the outside and in to Packleader again. He is sitting up a little. His face is all screwed up and he smells Much Hurting. Oh poor dear Packleader. I will lick your face again.

Packleader pushes me away. 'OK, Jack, now listen up. You see my coat over there.'

He is pointing with his paw at something, I do not know what. 'My mobile's in the pocket. You've gotta get it for me. OK, boy? You understand?'

No, Packleader, I do not understand at all. What do you want?

'Fetch,' says Packleader. 'Fetch coat. Fetch, Jack.'

What does he want? Oh maybe he is feeling tense in his tummy and wants something to chew. *Here you are, Packleader, here is a nice bit of wood for chewing, mind the splinters.*

Packleader puts it down. 'No, Jack, fetch coat.'

Another piece of wood?
No.
A nice stone?
No.
I'm very sorry if you're hungry, but Petra has eaten all the rabbit, I think. Shall I see?

I run round to upstairs, have a look. Petra is snoozing with the puppies. There is a bit of rabbit leg left. Pick it up carefully, bring it round back to Packleader. There you are, Packleader.

No? Why not? It's a very nice rabbit leg. Oh well, if you don't like nice fresh rabbit leg, I will eat it.

Crunch crunch. Now I will lie next to you, Packleader, keep you warm, make sure you don't get lonely, make sure Petra remembers you are my Packleader. Guard you from unfriendly NotMyPack apedogs. I don't think you are OK to fight them, you know. Never mind. I will guard you, keep you safe.

Oh. You want more fetching game? Why? Aren't you tired? You smell tired. How is your leg?

Oh. Sorry.

Fetch what? More wood? No. Another stone? No.

This is hard, Packleader. I want to do what you want but I do not understand what that is.

Fetch? Fetch coat?

What is 'coat'?

Packleader throws a bit of wood on something over in the corner. I fetch it for him. Is this what you want, Packleader?

He throws again. I fetch again. He keeps saying, 'Fetch coat.' I fetch the wood. Here you are. Why do you want to play this game, Packleader? Shouldn't you go to sleep? You smell tired.

No, this is a boring game, I don't want to play any more. Drop wood. I will lie down next to you.

Packleader will not rest like he should. He is trying to pull himself out of all the bits of wood. He is saying bad words, lots and lots and lots, but he is not angry with me, I don't think. He is saying I am Thick. Thick is Good. But his voice is sad and frightened-sounding. Oh dear.

Maybe he is angry with me. I'd better not be too near. Maybe the hurt is making him snappish. He gets a long bit of wood, he is trying to bash his removable fur with it.

Oh, I see, you want to kill the removable fur? I wonder why. OK, Packleader, I will help. Here we are, here is the removable fur, I will drag it, shake shake shake like I did with the rabbit. There, it's safe now.

Packleader is making funny noises: he gets the side of the removable fur and pulls it, finds the pocket. Oh dear, he is saying bad words at me.

What dropped when I was shaking it?

What is mobile? What? What do you want?

Do you want the talkbone?

Oh, you do? Why? Oh OK. I will bring it in my mouth.

Pad pad.

DROP.

'Good dog, Jack. Good dog.'

Pant pant. Packleader is pleased with me now. I am a Happy Dog. I am very Thick. He said so. Pat pat. More patting please, Packleader?

Now my Packleader has got the talkbone, his fingers are shaking and he does the ping pong peee thing. The talkbone says,

SSSHSSSSSS KKKKKKKKRRSSS.

I bark. I didn't know bad Cats could get into talkbones.

Packleader shakes it. Tries again.

SSSSSKKKKKKKKK Tries again.

SQUUUEEEEEEEEEEWKKKK.

Packleader puts it down, leans his head back. 'Blast!'

The talkbone didn't do what my Packleader wanted. Bad Bad talkbone. I will teach it a lesson, I will make it into meat, like my rabbit.

I bite it and shake it to make it stop the funny noise. Packleader yelps. Tries to catch it. Oh game, good game, play rag with the bad talkbone . . .

Scrunch, CRACK.

Oh dear. Talkbone fell in two bits.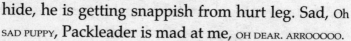

Packleader is shouting at me, he is very angry. I will hide, he is getting snappish from hurt leg. Sad, Oh SAD PUPPY, Packleader is mad at me, OH DEAR. ARROOOOO.

Whoops. Mustn't wake the puppies or Petra will be mad.

Everything is very complicated. Packleader has stopped being mad. Now he is lying back with the removable fur over him, shivering. He is cold and sad. Poor poor Packleader, I want to kiss you better, make you feel comfy and not lonely. Is it OK to come close now? Look, paws-up? Respect?

Oh good, Packleader is patting my head, stroking ears. Lie down next to him very carefully, not to hurt, cuddle up, keep him nice and warm. Soon it will start getting dark. Time for sleep, Packleader.

KABOOOM! YIP! YIP!

Packleader won't rest properly. First he does scratchy stuff with a snail-trail-stick from his removable fur. He is talking to me. He is saying nice things to me. He has torn off a bit of his shirt and tied it round my collar. Packleader is being most peculiar. Mostly it is bad to tear removable fur.

Now he is saying hard stuff again. 'Go home, Jack. Go home. Make like Lassie, you dumb dog. Go home.'

What is he saying? I will never abandon my Packleader when he is weak and hurt. That would be terrible. NotMyPack apedogs might come. Never never would I do such a bad thing.

'Go home, Jack. Suppertime.'

What? This is a very important word. Suppertime means Food. But there is no Food Dish here. How can I have supper? Here is another nice bit of wood for you, Packleader, is that what you want?

'Go home, get supper. Off you go.'

It would be nice to have suppertime. My tummy is a bit growly, though not as hungry as it usually is when it's suppertime. And it is suppertime, that's true.

'Go home, Jack,' says my Packleader. 'Go get supper. Off you go.'

He keeps saying it over and over. It makes my head hurt. It keeps reminding me about supper and my beautiful Food Dish.

But Packleader will be lonely if I leave him.

It's all right, says Petra. *I will make sure your Packleader is OK, so long as he doesn't come near my puppies. You can go home and get supper and then come back and unswallow it for me.*

That's a good thought.

OK, I will go home and get my supper. *Bye bye, Petra, take good care of my Packleader and the puppies.*

I think I will say hello to the nice woolly friends

150

on my way, so I will take the long way round by the road.

Pad pad. Follow my own trail.

Scrabble, scrabble, over the wall. *Hi, woolly friends, how are you, shall we play chasing games, I only want to be your friend* . . .

ROOF ROOF ROOF ARRROOOF.
Why are you running away?

KABOOOOM!

What?

KABOOOOM!

YOWCH, YELP YELP YELP . . . Oh OH Oh something bit me, something stung me, OH OH OH, SOMETHING HURT MY TAIL . . .

YOWCH,

roundandround and RUN round and bite tail, lick tail

Run
RUN
RUN
RUN,
get away from hurt, yowch yelp
help help help.

PACKLEADER HELP HELP
HELP!

Runrun run through brambles and nettles,
whoops, something came off. I wonder what. My
collar? Oh dear oh dear oh dear . . .

OH NO, THERE IS JACK BLOOD, I
CAN SMELL IT, IT MAKES ME ALL
SCARED AND FRIGHTENED AND
MY FUR IS UP, OH OH WOW
WOW WOW WHAT
SHALL I DO . . . ?

Quick! Find Packleader, he will make the hurt better, run run run quick. All the way along the road . . . OH OH OH HELP HELP YELP PACKLEADER, make it better, poor puppy, hurt puppy, yowch!

Run
run
run . . .

Here is my den, Packleader will help, he will make the hurt get better . . . Run in my den. Door shut! Oh no.

ROOF ROOF WARROOOF. ARROOOOF.

OK, have to make the door wood go away with my head. Run run run

kerbang!

Why is my head hurting too?

OK, back back, run run run . . .

whoops.

Oh dear. Suddenly the door was not there and the Pack Lady was and . . .

bonk.

My head rammed right into her tummy.
She said, 'Oof,' and sat down.

Oh, hi there, Pack Lady, so lovely to smell you again, how are you? Are you OK? Are you not so mad at me any more? Lick face, lick ears. Hi, hi, can I smell your . . . ?

Oh. Sorry.

BAD WHITECOAT APEDOG

Oh, this is so nice. All the puppies are yelping and shouting my name. They are cuddling me and patting me. Oh lovely. Paws up, show tummy, they pat my tummy lots and cuddle me. Terri is doing ape-type howling with water in her eyes . . . Why?

Pack Lady has gone to look out the door. 'Tom?' she calls. 'Tom, are you there?'

No, Pack Lady, Packleader is not here. I wonder where he is? There is something about Packleader which is worrying me, but I can't remember what.

Also I have a hurty. Make it better, please.

Look LOOK.

'Mum,' says Terri, 'Jack's bleeding. Look.'

Pack Lady comes back, her body says: *Worried, distracted, where is my Packleader?* 'What?'

'His tail's got lots of sort of little holes in it.'

'What? Let me see.' Pack Lady looks at my tail. I try to stop wagging but I am so happy to see her. Her face goes pale, she smells scared. 'These are shotgun pellets. Oh my God.'

Now she will help the hurty.

No. What is this? She is picking up the talkbone, she is doing the pawing thing but her clever paw is not very steady. She waits and waits but nothing happens.

Then she tries again. 'Police, please,' she says.

All my Pack go suddenly quiet and watch. What is happening, Pack Lady? Pant pant. Are you going to make my hurt get better?

Long wait. 'Yes, my dog's just come home on his own with shotgun pellets in his tail. My husband went out a few hours ago to look for him and he's not come back yet. Well, yes, I am worried. He'd normally have called by now to let me know what he was doing, but he hasn't. And his mobile's not working.'

More talking. Why doesn't Pack Lady do something about my tail? What about my suppertime? Arroooof!

I will go fetch my Food Dish. **Kerlang CRASH.** There, Pack Lady, do you remember now?

No, she doesn't. She is too worried. Oh dear. Am I a Bad Dog?

'OK. Thanks.'

Please, Pack Lady, can I have my supper now? KERLANG boing.

No, Pack Lady is doing talkbone stuff again.

Kerlang crash?

This is terrible, why won't Pack Lady feed me? Why is Terri-puppy doing water-howling again? And Pete and Mikey. What's going on? Is this a Pack Howl? It must be. OK, I'll help.

AROOOOOO. ARRROOOOOO. ARROWF ARROWF, ARROOOOOO!

157

Oh dear, I wish Packleader would come home, he will make it better. I wonder where he is.

That must be why we are doing a Pack Howl. We are howling so that Packleader can hear and come and join us. Louder, Packmembers, so Packleader can hear!

ARROOOO ARROOO ARROWF ARROWF ARROOOOOOOO!

Pack Lady is talking to the talkbone. 'Shut up, you stupid dog . . . Animal clinic? Yes, it's Charlotte Stopes. You remember my big yellow Labrador? He's come home with shotgun pellets in his tail. Do you know who might have shot at him? Yes, I know, but my husband went out to look for him because he'd run off but Tom's not back yet . . . Yes, OK.'

The talkbone goes back in its nest. 'Now, Terri, once the policeman has seen Jack's tail, I want you to take Jack round the corner to the vet's surgery, so he can get the shotgun pellets out. Can you do that?'

'What if I meet Dad on the way?'

'OK, maybe something's happened to his mobile, or he's run the battery down again. You take mine and DON'T LOSE IT, and if you find Dad, give me a ring, OK?'

Still no supper. Why not, Pack Lady?

There is a car stopping by our den. OH DEAR, maybe it's a NotMyPack apedog coming to get us? ARROOOF ARROFF ARROOOOF!

It *is* a NotMyPack apedog, very big, male, dark removable furs, has been eating biscuits.

The NotMyPack apedog comes in. ARROOOF ARROOOF. You can't have this den, this is my Packleader's den. He'll be back soon and he's very Big and Fierce. ARROOOOF!

Now he is patting me and saying nice things to me. I can smell that he likes me.

Oh OK.

Hi there, hi, pleased to meet you too, you are Big but friendly, you can pat my tummy.

Now he is looking at my sore tail. Yowch YELP.

'I see why you're worried, ma'am,' says the new apedog friend. 'He's just been caught by the outer spread of a shotgun blast. But if your husband was hurt, would the dog leave him?'

'If he was scared. He's not very bright.'

'Well, he's a lovely dog. I'll call the station and the hospital for you, ma'am, and I'll make sure the patrol cars know to look out for Mr Stopes.'

'Terri and Pete,' says Pack Lady, 'would you take Jack round to the vet now, please, so he can have his tail seen to?'

Terri and Pete don't really want to go out when their Packleader is lost, but Pack Lady has a *don't-argue-with-me* sound in her voice. So there is running around looking for paw-coverings and warm removable fur. Terri gets to hold the other carrying talkbone because she is the oldest.

She gets the lead off the hook. OH WOW WOW, HAPPY PUPPY! *Oh* GREAT, Terri puppy, CAN WE GO WALKIES, WALKIES NOW? It's a pity about supper, I really need supper, but can we go WALKIES,

160

that would be almost as nice and maybe I could find some chips at the bus stop again.

OK, lead on, off we go. Pant pant, bye now. Pant pant, sniff, snortle. Wet Message: *I am a Big Strong quite Fierce Packleader-type dog.*

Round the corner, sniff sniff . . . Bad smell.

Oh NO. I know that smell. There is the Bad Horrid hurty place where the apedog with the Whitecoat lurks. He is just waiting to grab me and poke my tummy and make me eat funny round pebbles and STICK HORRIBLE SHARP CLAWS IN ME . . .

I'm not going there!

CUDDLE PACKLEADER

Oh no, no, no, Terri, no, no, Pete, we're not going there ... **RUN RUN RUN** away from Bad Hurty horrible place ... pull pull on lead, you mustn't go in there, I don't want to go in there, come on, I'll save you from the Bad Hurty Whitecoat apedog, he is an enemy apedog, he is even worse than Garage Dog, he has dangerous sharp claws ...

Cats hate him too.[1]

---

[1] Why our apecats occasionally take Us to this evil apecat in his white coat nobody really understands. It's something to do with having bad paws, or feeling sick; he likes to poison weakened Cats with bad-smelling airs and then rip them with his claws while they're asleep because he is too cowardly to try and kill Us when We are well. This is another good reason for YOWLING AS LOUD AS POSSIBLE when apecats put us in the barred box and make us go in the horrible car.

Let's go this way, come on, Packmembers, come on, he'll catch you if you don't...

WHAT'S THIS? I can smell Packleader's smell in the air. It's coming from the same place as Petra and her puppies. Packleader's smell is frightened and sad and HURT.

OH NO. I remember now. Packleader has a bad leg. Packleader fell when the stairs turned into sticks.

Oh gosh. I must get to Packleader quick. That's why he couldn't come to the Pack Howl – his leg was bad. Oh dear. Oh dear. Can't you smell him, Terri? Can you smell him, Pete? Your Packleader is in trouble. Come on, let's go and help him.

Come on, Pack, this way. No, not a Bad Dog, Good Dog, we've got to go and keep Packleader warm and comfy so he doesn't get worse. He has a bad leg.

Oh dear, my Packmembers do not understand. They think I am only scared of the horrible Whitecoat apedog. Terri keeps pulling my lead, so I take it in my mouth. Come on, Terri, you come with me. Can't you smell your Packleader?

ARROOOF. ARROOOF. He's there. Look, I'm pointing with my nose. Come on, Terri. Come on, Pete. You know what I mean. You're my best friend. Come on.

Pete's coming with me; he understands. He keeps saying about 'Lassie'. What is a 'Lassie'? Food, maybe?

At last Terri's coming. She is frightened, it's beginning to get dark, but we won't bother the nice Woolly Friends this time because they have a Terrible Hurty Kaboom living near them and they're probably all meat now.

Along the path, come on, Terri, come on, Pete, mind the stream, whoops, never mind, you've got good paw-coverings.

Arrooof, Petra, here I come, sorry, no supper in my tummy for you, but I'm bringing Packmembers, they won't hurt your puppies, promise!

I take them round and through the door. Where is Petra? And what is the funny noise over by the road? I can smell NotMyPack apedogs again.

Pull Terri in through the door, she doesn't want to go, very gently get her removable fur with my teeth, pull pull . . . She stops, stumbles, blinks. Pete peers past her. 'Jack, what are you . . . ?'

Smell him? Can't you smell him? I know it's quite dark, just sniff.

'Who's there?' It's my Packleader's voice.

Now Terri and Pete can smell their Packleader.

'DAAAAD!'

'Dad? DAD! Oh, Dad . . .'

They rush over, tripping on all the bits of wood. Packleader was making a pile of wood to keep himself calm. When he sees Terri and Pete, he yelps happily. Terri nearly falls over his bad leg and then hugs him. Pete hugs him too.

Oh how nice. Pant pant. Can I have a cuddle too, Packleader? Oh pat pat, lovely Pack cuddle, it is so nice to cuddle up to Terri and Pete and my Packleader, even if Terri is doing that weird apedog howly thing with water in her eyes. They do loads of fast talking.

Terri looks at my Packleader's swollen-up leg. 'Oh, poor Dad.' She gives Packleader her removable fur to keep him warm. She is a good loyal Packmember. Lean against her, groan because I am a Happy Dog.

'Where's Mum, Terri? Is she here? Did you get my message?'

'What message?'

'I wrote a note on a piece of shirt and tied it to Jack's collar. I thought . . .'

'No, no, Jack brought us. We were supposed to take him to the vet because of the shotgun pellets . . .'

'What shotgun pellets?'

'Isn't that what happened?'

'No, the stairs collapsed and I think I've broken my blasted leg.'

'When Jack came back with his tail full of shotgun pellets we thought you'd somehow been . . . been shot by somebody with a shotgun. We were so worried. Mum's talking to the police. We were supposed to take Jack to the vet but he brought us here instead.'

'Jack, you're a hero.'

Pat pat, stroke, OOOOOOHHHH so nice, I love you, Packleader, thank you thank you . . . Paws-up, stroke tummy. Pat pat. Oooooooooo. More? Can I have supper now? Food? I have a terribly hungry tummy . . .

'OK, honey, can you run back and get me an ambulance?'

'I can do better than that. Here.'

'Oh, thank God.' Packleader does paw thing with talkbone, but it makes SSSS KKKK KKK KK.

I growl at it. Bad talkbone, don't make noises like a Mad Cat. I will bite you and crunch you up, protect my Packleader from you.

'For God's sake, keep it away from Jack, he bust the other one.' SSSS KKKK KKK KK.

'It's charged up, I don't . . .'

'I guess we're in a stone structure, flowing water, that's probably interfering with the signal. OK, honey, go outside, ring home, tell Mum where I am and what's happened. Then call emergency services and get me an ambulance. Don't go out the front, something weird's going on out there.'

'What?'

'I'm not sure, I only just woke up. Listen. There's some heavy machinery arriving. Go on, call Mum.'

What is this? Terri is abandoning her Packleader. These apedogs don't understand anything. Never mind, me and Pete will cuddle up to our Packleader.

Pete's looking scared at Packleader's leg. 'Gosh,' he says. 'Gosh, it looks awful. Poor Dad. Does it hurt loads?'

'No. Well, a bit, but not too bad.' Packleader's body says: *Hurts lots, very bad hurt, but I don't want to scare my puppy.*

But what about MY puppies? I can smell them, but not Petra. I will go and make sure they are OK.

Packleader, I'm sorry, but I must go check the puppies.

Round the outside, up the hill. Here are the puppies all cuddled up warm together. Sniff chiff. They smell very beautiful.

GRRRR GET AWAY FROM MY PUPPIES!

Oh hi, my Pack Lady, I didn't know where you were, I was just checking the puppies were OK.

Oh, it's you, Packleader (small respect). Something bad is going on. There are metal monsters outside. I have been

168

watching them. There are NotMyPack Fierce apedogs and they are cutting down trees. The metal monsters might come for my puppies. I have to move them. You are my Packleader, you have to help me with my puppies.

But I can't leave my own Packleader.

Then I'll move the puppies by myself.

Oh dear, I don't know what to do. Petra goes in and picks up a puppy very softly in her mouth and walks off with it, holding it up high. All her fur is up, she looks very magnificent and she smells terribly fierce and motherish. I want to help her, but how can I leave my Packleader when he is hurt?

Oh dear, my head is hurting. This is very hard head stuff and there are no bubbles to help at all.

Pad pad pad, go back to my Packleader. This time he is not so snappish, though he smells hurty. He is telling Pete all about how Petra was barking at him and I went up the stairs to tell her he was a friend and the stairs collapsed. He is saying the ambulance will be there soon, and everything will be all right . . .

SUDDEN TERRIBLE

**VRRRRRRROOM
CHUGGA
ROOOOOAAAAARRR!**

Oh woo, awoop, yip yip, scary, scary, METAL MONSTERS ARE HERE?

THE ROARING IS COMING VERY CLOSE. IT IS LOUD AND FIERCE ROARING.

I run up and down.

ARROOOF ARROOOF, YELP YELP. I'm scared, Packleader, I'm scared of metal monsters.

Packleader is shouting. 'Hey, what on earth are you doing? Help help!'

Nobody can hear with the metal monster roaring. OH NO, THE METAL MONSTER IS COMING TO EAT MY PACKLEADER, IT WILL GRAB

HIM AND SHAKE HIM AND MAKE HIM INTO MEAT!

Oh no. WHAT DO I DO? I don't know what to do. All my fur is up, it is so scary, now it's dark. So so so scary. Where is Terri, what is happening?

OH DEAR OH DEAR. My Packleader is trying to get up on his good leg, Pete is helping, but it's very hard for him. He smells scared. He is scared of the metal monster too.

THE METAL MONSTER MIGHT EAT THE PUPPIES!

OH OH OH WOW WOW WAROOOF!

This is terrible. What can I do?

There is another head bubble. It says: *Go and fight the metal monsters.*

What?

Me?

Big HUGE METAL MONSTERRRS!!

I can't fight the metal monsters. Come on, Packleader, let's run away. Petra will come and deal with the metal monsters . . .

Packleader can't run. Pete is helping him stand up. Terri is out on the other side of the place, doing apedog stuff with the talkbone. Petra is busy with moving the puppies and she isn't back yet. There is only ME.

OH DEAR. I don't know how to be brave. Wet Message happens suddenly on the floor. I am very very frightened.

GROOORRRRR, WHINE, ROOOOOAR.

The metal monster bites a wall and breaks it. Bits of earth and rock fall down, RUMBLE WHINE **NEEEOOOOOOOO.**

**AROOOFF
ARROOOOF
GRRRRRR . . .**

You can't eat my Packleader and my puppies. You can't do that, metal monster. I will fight you. All my fur is up. I am

TWICE AS BIG.
I AM <u>VERY</u> <u>FIERCE.</u>

I run outside.

GRRRRRRR GRROWF GRRROWWWF AROOO AROOO GRRRRRRRROWWFF!

Metal monsters have big staring eyes that make long sticks of light in the dusk. I'm not scared of your staring eyes, Bad Metal Monsters, I WILL KILL YOU, I WILL MAKE YOU INTO MEAT (but not eat you, because metal hurts my teeth).

GRRRRRRRROWWF. GRRRRRROWF. BADBAD BAD. GRRRRROOOOFFF.

A metal monster stops and goes to sleep suddenly. A NotMyPack apedog gets out. He is surprised and angry, I can smell him, oh dear. IT IS THE FIERCE APEDOG WHO LEFT THE WET MESSAGE.

I'm scared, scared puppy. But he is threatening my Packleader and my puppies.

GRRRRRRRRRROWF! I WILL MAKE YOU INTO MEAT AND EAT YOU, BAD APEDOG, I CAN DO THAT, I KNOW APEDOGS ARE MADE OF MEAT. GRRRRR.

I can smell him. He is a bit scared OF ME! I am standing between the metal monsters and my Packleader and my puppies and all my fur is up and I am showing all my teeth and my eyes are little slitty eyes and I am getting ready to *TEAR HIS THROAT OUT!*

GFRRRRRRRROWF GRRRRRRRROWF GROWF!

He's coming nearer. OK, I'm not sure how you do it with apedogs but I remember MY RABBIT. I bet if I bite you Where It Hurts you will yelp and run away. Better stay back. I am Jack, old-fashioned yellow Labrador, I am a

FIERCE AND DANGEROUS DOG.

GRROWF! YIP YIP YIP!

Oh phew, here is Petra, now she is really Fierce, she is fierce and mothery and all her fur is up too and she looks *HUGE AND WHITE with VERY BIG SHARP TEETH* and she is growling fiercely at the metal monsters. They are braver than me. I would run away from Petra if she said stuff like that to me.

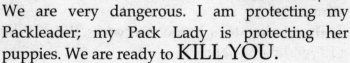

We are standing together. We are a Pack. We are very dangerous. I am protecting my Packleader; my Pack Lady is protecting her puppies. We are ready to KILL YOU.

Grrroooooowf!

Now the bad apedog has got a stick. He is looking fierce and scary.

'No, no. Wait! Wait!' Terri is coming to fight the metal monsters with teeth too, she is a very brave puppy, she is running up to the dangerous apedog and she is shouting, barking lots, very fiercely. 'My dad's in there, and my little brother. He's got a broken leg, and there are puppies. Stop, stop, you must stop!'

The apedog stops, he looks worried. 'What? What are you talking about?'

'And anyway, this is a site of special scientific interest, there's a protection order, you're not supposed to demolish it, what do you think you're doing?'

I can smell that his head is hurting, he is confused. Apedog girl puppies do not run around at night and suddenly appear from places he has brought his metal monsters to eat. He does not understand. 'It's none of your business, dear. Why don't you just control your dogs and run off home.'

Oh woww. He sounds very disrespectful and Terri is angry. If she had proper fur she would be all puffed up like Petra. She puts her hands on her hips. 'It is my business, because my dad's inside and he's got a broken leg and the ambulance is coming and my mum's coming and the police are . . .'

WEEAWWEEAWWEEEEAWWW . . .

Terri is standing in the middle, we are all three Big and Fierce with our fur up, METAL MONSTERS BETTER KEEP AWAY.

GRRRRRRRROWF!

Now the Bad apedog is scowling more, he is looking round, he is scared.

Cars are coming with flashing coloured lights, lots and lots, whirling round and round and yowling weeeaw weeaw. Petra is barking

177

more and more, I am barking. It is hard to hear anything.

BARK BARK BARK ROWWF GRRRRROWF BARK . . . !

'Shut UP, dogs, shut up!' roars Packleader from behind. He is standing on one leg, looking angry, all covered in bits of mud and wood and leaning on Pete, who is puffing because Packleader is jolly big and heavy, but he is <u>VERY</u> <u>VERY</u> <u>FIERCE</u> and he is ROARING BACK AT THE MONSTERS.

We are one very

FIERCE
AND DANGEROUS PACK.

'I know you, Joe Bristol, trying to wreck this place on a Sunday night so it can't get in the way of your blasted motorway.' Packleader smells very mad indeed. The enemy apedog is pretty brave not to do paws-up tummy for him. He just turns tail.

All the metal monsters stop and go to sleep. The apedogs inside climb out and get in a car. They drive off just as a white weeeawweeeaw bounces along the rough road and stops.

I GET STEAK!

There are lots of apedogs with dark removable furs and funny boxes and sticks. I go and stand next to Pete and my Packleader, who looks wobbly. Terri is holding onto Petra's collar which is quite brave of her, because Petra thinks the weeeawws have come for her puppies too and she is growling and snarling and yipping. You wouldn't believe the bad things she is saying to the apedogs in the weeawaw cars.

Packleader grabs my back, he is too wobbly, he has to sit down, and I break his fall. That's OK, Packleader, you are not that heavy. Here, you lie down and have a nice rest here. OK, that's better.

Pat pat pat. OH lovely. Packleader, why are you going to sleep now? The weeaw might get you.

Grrrr.

THERE ARE BAD NOTMYPACK APEDOGS COMING TO GET MY PACK-LEADER.

GRRRRROWF  GRROWF, BARK BARK, SNARL, GRRRRROWFFF!

Stay away from my Packleader, Bad NotMyPack apedogs. You can't touch my Packleader while he's sleeping, you can't disturb him, he needs to rest, he has a bad hurty, you can't come anywhere near

grrrrrrRRRROWF.

I AM A **BIG** <u>FIERCE</u> <u>DOG</u> AND ALL MY FUR IS UP!

Oh hi, Terri, are you going to fight the weeawaw apedogs too?

'It's OK, Jack, they're friends. They've come to help. It's OK, good dog, good dog. Come on, come this way, have your lead on. There.'

OH NO! The bad apedogs are putting my Packleader on a sort of bed of sticks, sticking sharp pointy claws in him! I will stop them, I will bite them Where It Hurts and . . .

Oh dear, Terri, I didn't mean to pull you into a thornbush. Oh? Is it really OK? Are you sure?

Pat pat pat. OK, if you say it is all right for the NotMyPack apedogs to take my Packleader away, maybe it is OK. Now they are taking him to the white weeawaw. Here is my Pack Lady and also Petra's John.

Am I a Bad Dog?

No. I am a <u>Good</u> <u>Dog</u>. Everybody is saying, Good Dog, Good Dog, pat pat pat.

Lots of patting in the car.

Lots of patting at home. Lots of people.

Whew. Now I am Happy Dog. Happy, happy!

My Packleader is back. He is OK now except he has got a funny white hard thing on his sore leg which I have to bark at whenever I see it.

He says we can have the puppies in our den, right here. And Petra too, of course![1]

Ow wow! Happy Dog.

My Pack Lady gets a BIG STEAK out of the Cold Cupboard and then SHE PUTS IT IN MY SUPPER DISH.

OH WOW? FOR ME? REALLY?

She says, 'Good dog, eat!'

HAPPY.

Yum yum YUM SLURP GULP GULP GULP.
Erp.
More?

THE
END

JACKSPEAK: ENGLISH

B between–ears face   forehead
    Big Furry–with–   horse
       hard–clip–clop paws
    Big Hunt   supermarket shopping
    Big White Water Dish   toilet

C Cats' God   fire
    car–blood   oil
    car–juice   petrol
    clicky–clacky Flicker Box   computer
    Cold Cupboard   fridge
    cow–milk–with–not–true   milkshake
       –fruit–taste

D den   where Jack lives, house
    Den That Moves   moving van
    Dog&Bitch game   mating

F Falling Over Juice   wine or beer
    Flicker Box   television
    floor–furs   carpets
    Flying Featheries   birds
    food–holders–on–wheels   trolleys

	food–skin	packaging
	Funny Pricklies	hedgehog
G	ground–up seeds	flour
H	hard cow–milk fat	cheese
	Hard Message	poo
	hard–shelled food	tin
	hot brown drink	coffee
	howling banging box	portable stereo
	Huge Great food Place	superstore
K	Kennel That Moves	car
L	leg–coverings	trousers
	lightning box	camera
	light–tree	lamp post
	Little Crawlies	insects
M	making into meat	kill
	Medium Eatable Furries with Long Ears	rabbits
	mouth–happy–squeaky –thing	squeaky plastic hedgehog toy

N	NEEEOOWWW things	jet planes
	nest	bed
	NotFetch	you fetch the stick, and then forget to bring it back
	not—trees with water—snakes	petrol pumps
O	old—milk—in—little—cups—with—fruit—in	yoghurt
	Outside	garden
	Outside Outside	everywhere else
P	pawball	good game involving ape puppies kicking a ball, Jack pawing it, and then Jack biting it until it turns into a rag
	paw—coverings	shoes/boots/socks
	piled—up—bread	sandwich
	pre—chewed cow—meat	mince
R	Ready	in season
	removable furs	clothes
	roaring—sucky—tube	vacuum cleaner
	round tick—tick thing	clock

RRRR–thing	lawnmower
Running Around Shouting House	school

S

sad hard place	boarding kennels
singed bread	toast
Slimys	frogs
Small Fierce Brown Wild Dog	fox
Smaller Fierce Stripy Face	badger
Small Furries	mice, voles, hamsters etc
snail–trail–stick	pen
Special	pregnant
Special Messages	puppies
strong–smelling pinky–red fish	smoked salmon

T

talkbone	telephone
Terrible Hurty Kaboom	shotgun
touching–paws–friendly–thing	shake hands
two–wheel–go–fast–thing	bike

U

unswallow	vomit

V	Very Big Funny Tasting Wet That Goes Whoosh Whoosh	the sea
W	water–howling	crying
	Water NotFurries	fish
	water–running	swim
	weeaweeaw cars	police cars/ambulance
	Wet Message	wee
	Whitecoat apedog	vet
	wood–and–metal–pling–plong–noise–thing	piano
	woolly friends	sheep

ABOUT THE AUTHOR

Jack Perry was born near Plymouth on the 7th April 1993, the only pup in his litter. After a brief time with someone else, he was adopted (at great expense) by the Perry Pack and their Owner, Remy.[1] Jack has moved dens twice and went to obedience school in Camborne where he was not at all obedient and far too friendly. His interests include eating, walking, food, swimming, break-fast, playing paw-ball with his Pack, supper, playing NotFetch and, of course, food-theft. He is an accomplished cereal-killer, dustbin-desperado and birthday-cake-bandit. Apart from this, however, he is mostly a Good Dog and is very gentle with everyone.

---

[1] Nobody asked ME. Remy

Patricia Finney is Jack's real Pack Lady. She spends a lot of time running around after Jack, the Cats, her three children and the Packleader. When she can, she writes all kinds of things including historical novels, scripts and articles for newspapers (winning the David Higham Award for her first novel), despite the Cats' constant attempts to stop her by marching across the clicky-clacky Flicker Box's keyboard and making it

crash
hhhh<>%^$£*&^

hhhh<>%^$£*&^